Book 3
Earth to Centauri

Black Hole: OBLIVION

Kumar L

Kumar L
Writer of Science Fiction and Fantasy

Earth to Centauri: Black Hole Oblivion

This edition first published in 2019

ISBN (Paperback) 978-9353822408

Edited by Vrinda Baliga (vbaliga@gmail.com)

Printed and distributed by Red Knight Books for and on behalf of Kumar L.

RED KNIGHT BOOKS

Books in the **Earth to Centauri** series

Book 1 – The First Journey

Book 2 – Alien Hunt

Book 3 – Black Hole: Oblivion

Book 4 – Civil War (to be released)

Short stories collections:

'8 Down' from Saharanpur—A collection of stories to touch your heart

Deceptions of tomorrow—Electrifying tales of science fiction

Non-fiction:

One Step at a Time: Your Self-publishing Master Plan

ABOUT THE AUTHOR

Whether you want to discuss faster-than-light travel, time travel, black holes or just the latest mobile phone, Kumar is your person.

He is a tech enthusiast and social media newbie. He enjoys travelling and is fluent in several languages. A mechanical engineer who loves pulling apart gadgets and exploring their innards, he writes science fiction stories and tries to bring future technology alive in his books.

The First Journey is the first book of the *Earth to Centauri* series. It is easy to read and understand and is suitable for all age groups. *The First Journey,* and *Alien Hunt,* the second book in the series, are both based on themes of adventure, thrill and drama, with a positive outlook at what the future may hold for humanity. *Black Hole: Oblivion* is the third book in the series with the latest adventure of Captain Anara and her crew.

He has also written a collection of short science fiction stories – Deceptions of Tomorrow – Robots, Black Holes & Time Travel.

You can reach him on:
Twitter @Captain_Anara
Instagram @KumarLAuthor
www.facebook.com/kumarlauthor

Visit his website www.kumarlauthor.com to get interesting news in the domain of science and technology, to avail special offers, and to stay updated on latest releases.

THE STORY SO FAR...

In the year 2117, *Antariksh* became the first spacecraft from Earth to reach the planet HuZryss four light-years away, in the Alpha Centauri Tri-Star system. Its captain, Anara, discovers two worlds—HuZryss and KifrWyss. HuZryss is a desolate planet, except for one settlement of 'new humans'. These 'humans' were born from the embryos carried aboard the Voyager probe, and raised by the reptilian civilisation of the planet KifrWyss.

Anara finds an enemy in the TrueKif, led by the enigmatic 'Chairman', who want to keep the KifrWyss reptilian bloodline pure. She and her team are held hostage on HuZryss, but they turn the tables on the Chairman with the help of nuclear weapons and a new ally, RyHiza, who is the leader of the ruling 'Discat' on planet KifrWyss. Anara and her crew return to Earth with three 'new humans'—Joe, Lucy, and her unborn child—who seek their help.

The Chairman hatches a plan to avenge his humiliation and dispatches two mercenaries to Earth with a deadly device, powerful enough to wipe out the megacity of Mumbai. Captain Anara, her crew and the NIA foil this plan, but they pay a hefty price; Anara loses her security officer and friend, Major Rawat. The main perpetrator of the foiled attack, Jim (a 'new human'), escapes, leaving his daughter behind.

There is, however, further peril in store for Earth—Jim explodes the device in space and the resultant explosion creates a black hole whose close proximity threatens the entire Solar System.

By the time people on Earth even become aware of this new menace, it may already be too late for humanity...

AUTHOR'S NOTE:

The pronoun 'it' has been used in this book for the reptilian people from KifrWyss, rather than 'he' or 'she', since they do not have gender differentiation.

CONTENTS

PROLOGUE

"Forty-four people are confirmed dead in the attack on the Indian Naval Hospital Ship, INHS Asvini, late last night. Another seventy-six were injured, twelve of them critically. The police have stated that the incident has been contained and the attackers have been neutralised. The identity of the attackers and their motives have not been divulged though initial reports suggest that two, possibly three, individuals were involved. Swift action by the NIA and the Anti-Terrorist Squad helped prevent further casualties. We are waiting for further details and will keep you posted as the story develops."

"In related news, the Commissioner of Police for Mumbai has stated that the complete loss of ComNet communications yesterday was a strategic decision by the NIA to locate and destroy the alleged terror cell involved in the incident at the INHS Asvini. The

Opposition has demanded a detailed inquiry into the incident, with special focus on the method employed which, according to them, 'violated the fundamental right to privacy of citizens'. They have also demanded an enquiry into the unconfirmed reports that the terrorists at the hospital were, in fact, aliens and that the whole incident is tied to the return of our spaceship *Antariksh* from Alpha Centauri. The Prime Minister is slated to address the nation in a short while from now. Stay tuned for this and other developing stories."

Superintendent Abhiram waved his hand to mute the news being relayed on every TelNet station and media channel. The ComNet was still down, though the system provider had promised to get it up and running by the end of the day and people were being provided with alternate communication patches. With the news muted, the sudden silence weighed heavy in the recovery room broken only by the soft beeps from the medical instruments.

He looked at the prone figure of Tejaswini Kaur, his boss and the Director General of the National Investigation Agency. Being shot trying to prevent an alien from annihilating the city of Mumbai; that was a first for anyone in the NIA. It had been a close call, but the doctors had managed to pull her through. Her injuries were no longer a threat, but she would need time to recover. He stared at the figures on the viewscreen and settled down again, resuming his vigil. He did not know what the future held for him or Tej, but he would come clean about the incident in Mumbai, the 'alien hunt' and the *Prana Protocol* if the investigators reached out to him.

His only consolation; they had made Earth safe. For now.

***

The tear in spacetime caused by the explosion of the TrueKif ship was hungry. It devoured all matter and energy within its reach and grew larger, forming a more substantial event horizon, the boundary from within which nothing could escape its hunger, not even light.

Its mere presence created a change in gravity. Like golf balls inexorably rolling down a dip in the golf course towards the hole at its bottom, all objects in its vicinity were drawn towards it. Very soon the black hole had a life of its own, feeding and growing. And yet it was invisible to everyone, just a deeper black against the emptiness of space. In the darkness, it waited, just beyond the solar system, insatiably hungry, waiting for its next victim.

1

The Estrangement

"The alien ship has escaped, sir. It accelerated to the speed of light before we could intercept it. Our sources inform us that the child and Captain Anara were left behind. They've been transported back to the hospital. We have managed to determine that there were two mercenaries. One was Jim, one of the new humans. It appears he was in collusion with the Chairman for the sake of his lovechild with Lucy. The second was a reptilian, Jur, likely one of the TrueKif terrorists who held Anara on HuZryss."

Jim was always the wildcard in the scheme. He and his partner had stayed hidden in the megacity, even managing to reach the hospital where Lucy and her child were kept, killing innocent people in the process. And after all this, Jim had managed to escape. 5 gritted his teeth. "What about the device?" Whatever else had transpired in the previous days, it was only the device that mattered. The device that, had things gone as planned, should have been in 5's possession by now.

"As far as we can determine, it was on the ship. It looks like Jim has taken it with him."

"We need that device, Henri. That was the agreement with the Chairman. We stay out of the way when they attack Mumbai and, if they fail, we keep the device. And now? Now, we have nothing. How did this happen?"

"We had no information of their plans, sir. There was just not enough time to get retrieval teams in place. I'm sorry Mr President, but I'm afraid the Chairman has double-crossed you."

"Double-cross? After a quarter century of contact?" 5 thought over the possibility, then shrugged. "We may never know for sure. What's important right now is that we get the device." He turned his sharp gaze on Henri. "I want that device, come what may. It will create a new future for our country. What are our options? Is the ship ready?"

"The prototype is ready, but we have never flown it beyond the solar system. The design has not been tested for longer journeys. We will be risking the ship and the crew."

"I'm sure our teams would want to be heroes. If the Indians can do it, so can we. No more tests. No more waiting. Get the team out now. Find and capture the TrueKif ship and bring it back to me!"

***

The holographic images of eight individuals filled the room, arranged in a circle, so each could observe, hear and talk to the others. These were the '8', successors to the Security Council, representing the most powerful nations on Earth in the twenty-second century.

"We were fortunate the aliens were captured before any further damage could be done," said 2, the Prime Minister of India, as he briefed the 8 about the failed attack on Mumbai. He was deep underground, in a secure communications room, dedicated exclusively to secure communications between the top leaders of the 8. The figures in front of him were detailed and realistic to the point that it was sometimes hard to remember that, in reality, each sat alone in a room identical to this one in some other corner of the planet.

"How many casualties?" asked 1, sipping from a coffee cup emblazoned with his coat of arms—an eagle.

"Forty-four dead, including one alien, and Major Rawat," replied the PM. "Jim, one of the new humans raised on the planet HuZryss, managed to escape. You will recall him from Captain Anara's reports from her mission. The second alien was a KifrWyss. A reptilian. Rawat killed him in hand-to-hand combat."

"A very brave man, Rawat." The President was genuinely proud of the Indian team, which had prevented a tragedy in Mumbai. "I'm sure you will honour the dead. Nevertheless, Jim escaped. And he still has the explosive device with him. We do not know how dangerous it is. The threat is still not over. We are sworn to protect Earth. We must do something."

"I agree. *Antariksh* is being readied for its next mission." There was a change in the PM's usually poised demeanour. "I will make them pay for every single life they have taken." His tone was controlled, but his expression betrayed him.

1 looked at him in alarm. "I hope you are not planning anything rash. Look where the TrueKif's

desire for revenge has brought them. We cannot become like them. We must show restraint."

The PM's anger finally burst through his controlled veneer. "No more restraint. No more talking. I have the means, and I will make them pay!"

"You are part of the 8, Mr PM. We will not allow you to destroy the peace we have worked so hard to bring to this planet. We are warning you."

The PM squared his shoulders. "Then it is time for us to part ways."

"You will break up the 8? For the sake of forty lives?" 1 was shocked. This had never happened before.

"It is not just about forty lives. We humans have become so accustomed to peace that we have forgotten how to wage war. The TrueKifs attacked my country! Sheer luck prevented a much larger catastrophe. I have the right to respond in kind and I will. They must now face my retribution. They started it, and now I will finish it. With or without your help. That's my promise!" The PM reached forward to terminate the transmission. "This meeting is over."

***

The Tri-colour fluttered lightly in the morning breeze, giving a glimpse of the wooden casket it was draped over. The dull finish of the wood belied the honour being bestowed by a grateful nation on the hero inside.

He died a hero, just the way he wanted to. It's a pity the world will never know about his sacrifice.

Anara stood in respectful silence in the cobblestoned yard of the crematorium, the morning drizzle doing little to calm the thoughts churning within her mind. Her crew had prevented a catastrophe, but their role in the entire episode of hunting the aliens would forever remain classified. A leak would result in a mob baying for the blood of an alien race, and a devastating interstellar war.

How much of this tragedy is my fault? I was overconfident to think I could take on the aliens. I am the captain of a spaceship, not a policewoman. If only I had been more restrained against Tej, Rawat might have been alive today. Yes, he died a hero, but was his death necessary? Did saving Lucy and her innocent baby justify my efforts? How was I to know Jim, of all people, would become the Chairman's tool and attack Earth? A lot of things did not make sense.

The remaining senior staff of *Antariksh* stood by Anara's side, their heads bowed in mourning. There were no words left to speak.

The *Pandit* chanted mantras for the peace of the departed soul. The body may be destroyed, but the soul lives on, he intoned.

Anara hoped the words of the prayers were true. She wished Rawat, who had thirsted for revenge ever since the episode on the planet HuZryss, had also found peace. It was less than a day since he had died fighting the TrueKif mercenary and she already missed his strength. There had been no time to say goodbye. Events had unfolded far too quickly. It wasn't until much later that Ryan had told her the complete story of Rawat's last stand.

Foolish but immensely brave.

As the body entered the incinerator, they stood in silence, in honour of the fallen hero. The time for explanations and anger would come later.

***

It was afternoon by the time Anara and Ryan managed to reach the Prime Minister's Office. The wood-panelled office was immaculately clean. It was empty except for the PM himself, seated behind his desk.

The Prime Minister rose as they entered his office. He walked around his desk and took Anara's hands in his own.

"I am sorry for your loss, Captain," he stated simply. "Major Rawat was a courageous man, and he died in the line of duty, protecting those he cared for."

Anara nodded, acknowledging the truth in words, yet finding no solace in them. She fought back her anger and tears, thankful that the PM had turned to shake Ryan's hand. He motioned them into comfortable chairs and settled himself behind the desk.

"But what's done is done. We must look toward the future now. The enemy has breached Earth and our country. You may have prevented them from carrying out a cowardly attack this time, but at a terrible cost. We cannot forgive them for the lives they have taken and the families they have destroyed."

Anara glanced up at the PM. Something had changed in him. She had been too wrapped up in her grief to have noticed at first, but now the change in his tone was unmistakable, and she suddenly found herself tensing in anticipation of what would come next.

"As of today, we are no longer part of the 8," the PM continued. "I have withdrawn India from the group. This is now our fight. Ours alone. We are now at war with the TrueKif terrorists and by extension perhaps with the KifrWyss world itself!"

Anara stared at him, shaken by the vehemence contained within his words. Was this the same person who had been advocating peace for so long?

"Too many times in the past have we given in to our fears and allowed our country to be complacent, only to be betrayed every single time. But never again!

The TrueKif want a war, well they've got one now. Do they want death? Then they will die. We will take this battle to their planet now!" He stood up, almost shaking with anger, all pretence of control evaporating from his body.

Anara struggled to prevent the alarm from showing on her face. What did the PM intend to do?

"I've ordered *Antariksh* to be prepared for a new mission," the PM went on, relentlessly. "Time is short. We must get your crew on board. You have two days to launch. Fortunately, our weapons are still on board."

Understanding dawned on Anara. She'd just become a pawn, a mere foot soldier, in a galactic war. Only, it wasn't just any war; this would be genocide.

"I'm afraid I don't understand, sir." She turned in her chair to follow his figure as he paced around. "Surely you're not referring to the nuclear devices? That would be insane!"

"Insane, Anara? Insane? Was it not insane, what they tried to do to our city? Was it not insane that they tried to destroy thirty million lives? No! This is not insanity! This is justice!"

"Justice? How is it justice to destroy a whole civilisation for the... the... the mistake of a few individuals?" She got to her feet. Ryan followed suit, keeping quiet for the moment. "An eye for an eye will make the world blind!"

"Don't try and get all self-righteous on me, Anara. Let me worry about the ramifications. Your job is to fly the ship." The PM stepped forward and came face to face with her. "Don't forget you're just a pilot."

Confusion gave way to raw fury and her face turned red. She looked at Ryan to steady herself before speaking, and she saw the same anger reflected in his face. Her thoughts became clear, and her resolve strengthened.

"Thank you for the confirmation, sir. Since I am only a pilot in your eyes, then I'm sure you will have no trouble finding someone to replace me on *Antariksh* to carry out this mission of yours. I resign my commission with immediate effect. I would rather die than carry out genocide."

With that, she saluted smartly, turned on her heels and stomped out. Ryan followed her without hesitation, leaving the Prime Minister fuming in their wake.

***

They exited the PMO and turned right down the wide Rajpath. They continued to walk in silence for nearly an hour till they reached India Gate.

The massive memorial to the 70,000 soldiers, who had died two centuries ago in the First World War as part of the British Indian Army, was surrounded by 3D holograms depicting scenes from the battles fought by the Indian Army in the years since. Children and adults alike participated in the virtual display with excitement.

Anara and Ryan joined the crowds in front of the Amar Jawan Jyoti, the eternal flame, a tribute to the Unknown Soldier. Thankfully, they had donned plain jackets over their uniforms, and nobody recognised them as they stood in comfortable companionship, watching the tongues of fire dance mesmerizingly in the twilight.

"Let's go sit over there on the grass, Ryan," Anara said, finally.

They navigated their way through the light traffic and sat down in the garden. The temperature dropped rapidly as the sun disappeared and dark shadows covered the ground. The Rajpath was a wide tree lined avenue flanked with gardens on both sides. Every summer evening, it turned into a large fair ground with families coming over to relax in the cool evening breeze. The sky above twinkled not only with stars, visible in the clear skies, but also with the blinkers from the mass of airborne vehicles and drones.

A few minutes later Ryan got to his feet and wandered off somewhere, but she did not mind. Anara enjoyed sitting alone in anonymity, watching the families frolicking around. The cool grass and the gentle breeze lifted her spirits, though she was still riled at the PM's attempt to browbeat her.

She watched as Ryan returned, bearing egg rolls, expertly dodging the children playing handball.

"Here you go," he said, handing her a roll and settling down on the grass beside her. He took a large bite from his own roll. "Man, I was hungry. This is good."

"By any chance, are you trying to cheer me up?" asked Anara as she tried her own roll. She was hungry too. She took another bite and looked at Ryan, waiting pointedly for an answer.

"Not really. I know you'll come around in your own time. I can't do anything to hasten up your complex thought process. I've known you long enough."

She did not answer immediately, trying to compose her thoughts. "He's changed, Ryan. I could not believe it was the same person who told me at our first launch two years ago, that we are going in peace into interstellar space. Now, I find he knew about the hidden nuclear weapons on my ship. At least, the last time we did not use the weapons except to threaten the TrueKif. But now? Now he's asking us to go to KifrWyss and wage war using nuclear bombs. What am I, his personal mercenary? No. We did the right thing walking out of there."

"The right thing, perhaps, but was it necessary to resign your commission? Wasn't that a bit extreme?"

"You supported me, didn't you? You walked out right behind me. If you didn't agree with my decision you could have stayed back." She was annoyed with his apparent lack of faith in her decision.

"And I support you now, but wasn't your reaction a bit extreme? Is provoking the most powerful person in India the practical way forward?" He was convinced about her decision, just not her means.

"I don't know," she sighed. "I still think it was the right thing to do. The KifrWyss are not at fault. RyHiza told us, didn't it, how they had raised the human children and taken care of their safety? How can we then think about punishing an entire planet for this attack in Mumbai? The attack was the handiwork of a few individuals."

Ryan nodded. But he still looked concerned. "What will you do now? You have no ship and no crew." He could always go back to the US, but he knew she was too deeply in love with space exploration.

She sighed. "Maybe I'll retire to my hometown, Kasauli, and start working on my memoirs."

"Yeah, be sure to let me know how retired life works out for you," he smirked. "You'll be out of your mind in no time and looking for your next space trip. I know you too well. I suggest you go and sleep over it."

She looked away. A mild breeze ruffled her dark hair and she put a stray wisp back in place. "Sleep won't come easy. I keep thinking about Rawat, and now more and more about RyHiza. It had asked me for help personally. I wonder whether it is still alive. God knows what the situation is on the ground on KifrWyss. The Chairman has proven that it is ruthless. It will not spare RyHiza. And now I have lost the only chance I had of going back and helping it. I… I really don't know if what I am doing is sensible. Sometimes our decisions continue to haunt us, no, however justifiable they may be?" Anara stopped speaking and was lost in her own thoughts.

Ryan let her be. *She needs time.*

***

It was past 1 a.m. when they walked back to their hotel. Their rooms faced each other on the same floor.

"Good night," Ryan called as she opened the door to her room. She gave him a cursory wave, closed her door and wearily leaned against it.

She tossed her jacket on a chair and threw herself on the bed face down. Tomorrow, she told herself. Tomorrow, she would pack and leave. She closed her eyes, willing her mind to rest.

She must have drifted off to sleep at some point, because the next thing she knew, the room AI butler was waking her up softly.

"Ms. Anara, you have visitors."

"Who is it?" she mumbled. "Tell them to come back tomorrow."

"I'm afraid that is not possible. It is the police. They have override authority."

"Override authority? Police? What do you mean override authority?" She raised herself from the bed. "Who is it?" she called out.

"Captain? Captain Anara?" a female voice came through the door.

"Yeah. What do you want?"

"You are required to present yourself at the PMO immediately."

"I have nothing to do with the PM or his office. In case you haven't heard, I have resigned and I no longer answer to that authority. So, go away."

"Captain, please open the door. We have orders to bring you with us."

Crap, she thought, her anger rising again as she stomped to the door and jerked it open. *He can't order me around, so he sends the police to arrest me?*

"I told you, ACP," she said, glancing at the stars on her epaulette and deducing her rank, "I don't have anything more to do with the man in the PM's office!"

"But...but... haven't you heard?"

"Heard what?"

"The PM was sacked a short while back for his role in the conspiracy. Apparently, they have evidence that he authorised the use of stealth-tracking of citizens during the terrorist attack in Mumbai. President's rule has been imposed and the Speaker of the Parliament is the new interim PM. It is she who has asked for you. I'm under orders to bring you in, no matter what."

Anara was stunned. Events, it seemed, were unfolding faster that she was able to cope up with. Ryan stepped out of his room just then, pulling her out of her reverie.

"Won't hurt to hear hearing what the new PM has to say, right? If it's more of the same, then you won't even have to resign again. You can just walk out," commented Ryan, his face deadpan. Anara raised her eyebrow at this weak attempt at humour.

"You have been summoned too, sir," the officer told him. "Please come with me. I have a vehicle waiting outside."

2

Compromises

The transparent canopy of the police car provided a wonderful view of the night sky and the multitude of airborne vehicles, even at that time of night. It took them less than five minutes to get back to the PMO, the central traffic computer having cleared a direct path for their police vehicle. Even at 3 a.m., the area outside the PMO was a hotbed of activity with news drones, bots, a few human reporters and their equipment jostling for vantage points, even as uniformed security personnel and security-bots held them back behind barricades.

Their vehicle turned left a little ahead of the complex, doubled back and landed at a relatively deserted side entrance. A waiting security guard led them indoors. The lateness of the hour and the stress of the last few days were finally taking a toll on Anara. She felt drained. She had no strength left to argue with anyone. She didn't know what the interim PM wanted from her, nor how she should react. One thing was clear, though, she would not participate in mass murder.

"Let's not linger, Ryan. We'll just let her make her pitch, nod our heads, say no, and get out of here. I've have had enough of politics. Can't they understand the TrueKif are our enemy, not the entire race of KifrWyss?"

"So, when you say nod the head and say no, you're actually referring to your great Indian head bobble, right? The PM would not know whether you're for or against her plan. Then you can get away with anything!" Too spent to even smile, she looked at him, shook her head in exasperation and strode on.

The secretary at the door to the PM's office ushered them inside immediately, disregarding the gaggle of senior bureaucrats and political officers waiting outside for an audience with the PM.

They entered the brightly lit room for the second time that day, to find the new PM staring out the windows at the garden outside. A number of viewscreens dotted the walls, displaying data or replaying the news mutely. The PM did not acknowledge their presence, and they stood waiting awkwardly.

Looks like it's going to be a passive-aggressive play. Okay then. Lead me on.

Finally, the secretary gave a small cough, and the PM turned around. Her visage gave nothing away. She nodded and the secretary turned and exited the room.

"Thank you, Captain Anara, for coming back. It has been a difficult day for our country. I have been briefed that you knew about the *Prana Protocol,* the attempt to invade the privacy of our citizens in Mumbai during the terrorist attack. It seems our ex-PM had authorised the use of the clandestine protocol even though it was illegal."

Anara and Ryan looked at her in silence.

Is this about punishing us for being part of the NIA team which broke the law?

"Be that as it may, a new interim government is in place now. I intend to carry on the task of my predecessor even while we wait for the final government to take shape," said the PM. "I'm aware it must be been difficult for you but as you have probably been told many times today, you're our only hope in these demanding times." Her voice was soft, controlled, though she looked as worn out as Anara herself felt.

"I don't think so, ma'am. There are quite a few pilots with ISC who can take my place." *Pilot is what the earlier PM had called her. Pilot, indeed!* "Besides, I'm sure they've told you that I resigned my commission yesterday. I can't help you anymore."

The PM smiled. "Unfortunately, Captain, you may have resigned but that doesn't mean you're no longer in service. There's the little matter of your resignation being accepted, and you being discharged from duty. Till such time, I'm afraid, you'll have to do as I say, unless you want to face a court-martial. Do you?"

Cat-and-mouse games. Alright. Up the ante.

"You've evidently thought this through, ma'am," she said calmly. "I'm ready for whatever charges you want to throw at me. But, let me make it clear once more—I will not be a party to the hair-brained genocide scheme of your predecessor. Clap me in irons if you must, but I will not do it."

The PM sat down behind her desk, regarding Anara with half-closed eyes. "Uh huh. I thought you'd have this reaction. However, I want you to hear me out first. All right?"

"As you've so elegantly stated, I'm still under your command. We'll listen."

"That's sufficient. I'm going to ask General Singh and Mr Arya to join us now. Have a seat, Captain. Commander."

The Chief of Staff of the tri-forces and the National Security Advisor. She's bringing out the big guns.

They had to only wait a few seconds before the two officials entered the room. The PM gestured them all into seats while she herself stood up and paced around. She gathered her thoughts before speaking.

“You may not be aware, Captain, but my predecessor has pulled India out of the 8. Our country now stands alone in this fight.” She glanced at the seated folks to ensure she had their undivided attention before continuing, “It is also important to note that I don’t agree with this decision, nor with his plan to wage war against the KifrWyss terrorists. However, we cannot allow this challenge from the TrueKif to go unanswered. You have to understand that we have to respond. That is why we are going to initiate plan B—the capture of the leaders of the TrueKif so they may be brought to Earth to stand trial for their crimes against humanity. It will require the help of the 8 of course, and for that I am prepared to go back and apologise for whatever has happened so far. But I need a solid plan first.”

The PM nodded to the general, who took up the narrative.

“We've been training a company of commandos for space travel and interplanetary warfare. This group is called Joint Interstellar Task Force, the JITF.

It is led by Colonel Alan Fraser of the British SAS. The soldiers have been drawn from the best special forces around the world—the British Special Air Service, the US Navy SEALS and the Indian Navy Marine Commando Force, MARCOS. They are ready for deployment. We are going to deploy five sections, fifty troopers, for Mission Trikon. They'll travel with you to KifrWyss, locate and neutralise the TrueKif and capture their leaders."

"Sounds like a great plan, General." Anara couldn't hide the sarcasm in her voice. "Fifty soldiers on an unknown world to find one set of people. I'm sure that'll be a cakewalk."

The NSA smiled. "That's why it's important that you are part of the mission, Captain," he said. "You have first-hand knowledge of the planet and its people. More importantly, when RyHiza faced a revolt it reached out to you. Clearly there is more at play here than just friendship. They need us, and our evaluation is that the Discat will be happy to receive any help we can give them."

"You're asking me to use my friendship with RyHiza and get it to help us wage war on its world? Have you lost your mind? Why would it do that?"

The NSA leaned forward. "They are desperate, that is why. You heard RyHiza's message. Our analysis has deduced that the Discat is under tremendous pressure. In fact, we believe that we might already be too late to help them. More than three months have passed since the message was received. At least eight months will pass before you reach Alpha Centauri again. Fortunes change daily in war. What do you think will happen over months?" The NSA glanced at the PM for support.

"Don't you want to help your friend, Captain Anara?" asked the PM softly.

They got her, thought Ryan. *She never lets her crew and her friends down. Never.* He could see Anara visibly wavering. *The strength of a leader is not how fast they hold on to their principles, but what they are willing to give up for their followers.* He thought she was a great leader, with some faults.

"And we will not be forced to carry or use nuclear weapons?" Anara asked. "Will you give us your word on this?"

The PM looked uncomfortable. "They will be only be on your ship as a deterrent. The weapons of last resort. You and only you, Captain, will have the launch codes. You can decide if you want to use them or not."

The deal was being sweetened.

"There will be no tactical orders from us. You will have absolute control over all aspects of the operation. Colonel Fraser will control the military ops. You only have one objective—bring back the Chairman to Earth, dead or alive."

This was not an operational decision. She had to trust her guts. She was torn between her desire to help RyHiza and punish the Chairman, and her hatred for nukes. Anara met Ryan's eyes and he gave her a slight nod of support. *Oh what the hell! In for a penny, in for a pound. Let's do this. Better than sitting at home writing memoirs.*

"I'll do it," she said.

3

Operation Trikon

The hangar on the moon base resembled a deep cavern. With just hours left before the launch, it was buzzing with activity. Anara strode in, trying to tune out the mechanical sounds and human chatter flooding the hangar. It had been a difficult two weeks for her and her team. There had been no time to mourn their fallen colleague and friend, there was just too much to do in the limited time available. The orders for the recall of the crew of *Antariksh* had gone out immediately after her meeting with the new PM. Operational briefings had begun within a few hours of the arrival of her crew.

The crew was mostly ready, but the condition of *Antariksh* itself was a cause for concern. It had been battered during its almost two-year journey to Alpha

Centauri and back. Additionally, in the last few months of its return journey it had been pushed to its limits and beyond. It had been taken into dock for overhauls soon after its arrival, but the new situation meant that it would have to go back into space much earlier than previously anticipated. Fortunately, ISC had managed to carry out major repairs even if it had meant gutting spare parts from the new ship *Antariksh-2,* still under construction. Anara trusted and hoped that the intense efforts over the last few days would be enough for her next journey.

***

Manisha stood in the large hangar watching the loading of the final set of supplies. She noticed a tall man in an unfamiliar uniform supervising a squad of soldiers similarly dressed.

So that is what the JITF looks like. Quite handsome. Major, huh? He obviously outranks me, but it wouldn't hurt to talk to him.

The loading seemed to be at an end, and she saw him dismiss his men and walk around checking the cables securing the cargo.

She stepped forward to where he stood and saluted. "Good morning, Major. Lieutenant Manisha. Conn Officer, on this ship."

He returned her salute. "Major Kevin, Lieutenant. US Navy SEAL and now with JITF. You're not the same intrepid Lieutenant who broke into the NIA's secure systems and helped save a city?" he asked.

"No one was supposed to know about that, and I did receive the President's pardon, so I'm good," she replied.

"We got a full briefing, you know, about the events in Mumbai when we were asked to prepare for this mission. It seems you were an all-out badass with a computer. Nice!"

He smiled, taking an immediate liking to the bright-eyed young woman. The strict regimen back at camp did not allow much time for socialising, and maybe it was time to make some new friends.

"Lieutenant Manisha to Ops, please. Lieutenant Manisha to Ops." The announcement came over the ship's speakers.

"Acknowledged," she said into her own radio. She looked back at him. "Sorry. Can't talk now. Duty calls." She started to walk away.

Uh-oh. Not so fast lady. "Um. I'm off to JITF centre myself. Maybe you can show me the way."

She smiled internally and nodded.

Kevin followed her. "Tell me, is it always so hectic on a spaceship?"

"Only during take-off and in these special circumstances. And, of course, when you are being shot at by enemy aliens or saving a city. Otherwise, it's quite dull."

I'm gonna like her, he decided.

They came to a T-junction in the corridor.

"The JITF centre is that way, sir," she said, pointing to the left. "And I will need to go right."

"Thanks. Maybe we can get together later for a drink or something?" he asked, hopefully.

"Sure, sir. I'll look you up. See you soon." This trip had just got more interesting, for her at least.

***

Anara felt a surge of pride looking at *Antariksh*. The ship seemed to beckon to her and her pace quickened as she approached it, eager to assume her command and get away from the political machinations of Earth. It would be good to get back in space. Space was dangerous. Space was unforgiving. But it was devoid of human deceptions and politics. She felt she needed the emptiness of space to regain her emotional balance. Within the cocoon of *Antariksh,* she could heal. Her ship loomed large in front of her.

Antariksh was 150 meters long, capable of housing a hundred people comfortably and had three levels. Level 1 at the top was the control section, with the Operations Centre or Ops in the front. The medical bay, engineering, observation and navigation systems took up most of the rear. Level 2 housed the crew quarters, communal areas, the cafeteria and the *dome.* Level 3 housed the power plant, standby generators, battery banks, solar power banks, antimatter storage, utilities and the escape pods.

Launched in the year 2096, it had taken fifteen years to build and another five years to test. Though Faster-Than-Light or FTL speeds had been made possible by 2085, sustaining the same for extended periods of time, and with humans on board, had required scientists to come up with path-breaking applications of quantum mechanics. Even so, it had taken nearly a decade for the management of power supply—with a combination of fusion reactions and controlled matter & antimatter explosions—to be perfected for practical use. To protect travellers from the time dilation experienced during FTL, the bubble-like *dome* had been constructed to enable a mix of suspended animation and isolation from all external references. In all, what stood before her was a marvel of science and engineering.

The ramp was open. As she entered the ship two junior officers stopped their discussion, stepped back and saluted smartly. She nodded her acknowledgement and climbed the stairs to the Ops Centre. She was not surprised to find the chaos outside the ship had penetrated all the way to Ops.

Her eyes sought and found Commander Ryan, surrounded by various section heads. Ignoring the rest of the crowd, she moved behind him and tapped him on the shoulder. Ryan turned around in annoyance, but his face immediately brightened on finding her onboard.

"Looks like you have everything in control, Commander," she remarked looking at his tousled hair and grimy uniform. Not how he looked most of the time. Thankfully, his discipline and drive had allowed Anara a few hours of rest and the time to make herself presentable.

Ryan sheepishly ran his hand through his hair, trying to finger-comb it into order. "Sorry, I've not had a chance to freshen up."

"Relax, Ryan. Just pulling your leg," she smiled. Then she slipped into her captain's role. "What's the status?"

"We are at 97% readiness. Just waiting for the last set of supplies to be loaded. The Joint Interstellar Task Force has brought a lot of equipment on board. Flying and tracked crafts, drones, heavy weapons, you name it. Our payload has gone up by almost forty percent. Add to that the fifty commandos, and extra fuel and food supplies, we are rolling heavy. Anyway, right now we are accounting for all the equipment and locking it down. We should be ready to launch on schedule."

"What about the Colonel and his team?"

"I've assigned them quarters and they're settling down. Colonel Fraser has requested a meeting with you at your earliest convenience."

"He has, has he? Well, the good Colonel will have to wait till we've launched. He's not my priority right now. How about you take a short breather and meet me back here in thirty minutes. In the meantime, I'll manage the tasks as hand." She held out her hand and Ryan handed over his data pad gratefully.

"Thanks. It wouldn't do for the people to see your second-in-command looking like he's been dragged through a pig pen." Ryan paused for effect. "And smelling like it too."

As he left, Anara looked around for Lieutenant Manisha to help bring her up to speed. There was much work yet to be accomplished before they could get underway.

"Captain Anara taking over from Commander Ryan. Note in the logs. Okay, Lieutenant Manisha," she addressed her conn officer or helmsperson, "let's do the next system-level status check. Proceed, please."

"Affirm, ma'am. Initiating second-degree system-level checks now. Estimated time to complete, one point five hours," confirmed Manisha.

Anara acknowledged her report. "Let me know once finished. We will be launching in three point five hours. Mr Madhavan?" She spoke next to her Engineering head over the intercom, "how're my engines coming along?"

Madhavan was moving around, seemingly at random, from station to station in Engineering, passing along instructions and checking readings from a dozen status boards simultaneously. This might have overwhelmed any other person, but he was in his element among his engines and the constant hum which seemed to pervade the atmosphere in Engineering.

"All boards are green, Captain. Matter-Antimatter, M-AM drive ready for operation. Fuel loading complete. Environment systems are green. We're good to go. Fusion engines will be at thirty percent power in one hour."

"Roger, Madhavan." Anara sat back in her chair and looked around the Ops Centre or Ops as they had come to call it.

A large holographic display in the centre provided them a three-dimensional image of space when they were flying. It would track and identify foreign objects and also display the flight map for the journey. Ops was surrounded on three sides by large portholes. While useful in observing outer space during sub-light flying, the portholes were useless at FTL or faster-than-light speeds. When *Antariksh* was in FTL flight, the portholes would convert to virtual windows displaying simulated images of the space outside.

Multiple stations around Ops controlled every vital function of the ship, but if needed one person was enough for navigation. And, of course, the ship's Artificial Intelligence, named Narada, was more than capable of handling the entire ship if the crew was incapacitated due to any reason. Having been given legal rights, Artificial Intelligence systems were given human names and assigned genders if they so wished. Narada had been named after an ancient Indian sage, regarded as wise, mischievous and someone who knew secrets. The AI lived up to the name.

During the first flight from Earth to Alpha Centauri, Narada had been found to be hiding the storage of nuclear weapons on the ship, from the Captain and the crew. Having faced a severe reprimand, he had been under observation for further signs of untrustworthiness throughout the journey. He had explained that his ethical programme had been deliberately tampered with by the DRDO when they placed the nuclear devices aboard *Antariksh,* but

Anara had been unwilling to rely on him till the battle on HuZryss, when he had regained his right to be treated as a trusted member of the crew.

"Narada, begin countdown to launch. Secure personnel. All senior officers to be in Ops by T minus one hour."

"Roger, Captain Anara."

"Manisha, give me the flight path data."

"Displaying on your screen now, ma'am."

A virtual display appeared in front of Anara and she used her hands to manipulate the image. The probable path taken by Jim during his escape from Earth had been plotted alongside. The problem was that space was just too enormous to be patrolled or covered effectively, even by the multitude of assets placed by humans across the solar system. Only one station, on Jupiter's moon Europa, had managed to track Jim as he had sped away from Earth. The TrueKif ship was somewhat faster than *Antariksh*, and the consensus was that *Antariksh* was at least ten days behind it.

Anara swiped her hand to transfer the data to the main holo-display, then sat back to study the ship and crew manifests. *Antariksh* was heavy with all the extra load added to it, but having been designed to hold a crew of a hundred people, it could handle the weight.

After all, it was the largest FTL-capable ship ever built for the purpose of interstellar travel.

We are as ready as we are ever going to be. Time for some action.

4

Reluctant Allies

The view of the rings of Saturn as *Antariksh* travelled past it at sub-light speed finally allowed Anara to relax. The events of the last few weeks back on Earth, had taken a larger toll on her emotionally than she cared to admit. Her mind continued to dwell on the loss of Major Rawat. It had taken only forty-eight hours between the landing of the mercenary TrueKif ship on Earth and the devastating firefight at the hospital. Jim had left his baby daughter in Anara's hands. She believed he regretted the havoc he had caused by submitting to the Chairman's will. She also believed that he could be reformed, if only she could reach him in time. The device he carried, which he had failed to blow up in Mumbai, was supposed to be more powerful than ten nuclear bombs. She had to find it and neutralise it. Otherwise there was no telling what destruction the Chairman could cause. Moreover, she and Ryan had practically had no time to rest or acclimatize to the new space journey. Here they were again, moving across space and time, going once more into the unknown. Nevertheless, she was a leader and she could not allow her emotional turmoil to come in the way of her duty.

Might as well get it over with. I cannot avoid meeting the Colonel any longer. After all, we are jointly in command.

She got up from her chair and gestured for Commander Ryan to follow her. "You have the command, Manisha."

Anara and Ryan exited Ops side-by-side, neither speaking for some time.

"Where are we going?" Ryan asked finally, as they went down the steps to Level 2.

"I thought we will pay a visit to the JITF and plan our next move. Did you get time to go through their mission profile?"

He nodded.

"And what do you think of it?"

"The intent looks good, but fifty troops against an entire unknown planet full of TrueKif terrorists? It's going to be suicidal," he said, blandly.

"We have beaten them twice before, haven't we? Once when we outwitted them to escape captivity on HuZryss, and then again back in Mumbai." She hoped she sounded confident even though she agreed with Ryan's assessment.

"We did locate and neutralize the aliens before they could do any major damage. That has to count for something," he agreed. "But, that was a piece of cake compared to our situation today. The entire military might of India was behind us at that time, not to mention the fact that it was our home turf. This is going to be way harder. It was only a city last time; this time around it is a whole damn planet!"

They had reached the JITF command post. She knocked and entered. Fraser got up from behind his desk and greeted them.

"Good of you to come over, Captain Anara," he said. "You have met Major Kevin of the US Navy Seals and Lieutenant Rana of the MARCOS earlier, I believe?"

Anara acknowledged the two soldiers who saluted her. They had met briefly at the mission guidance.

"Can we get down to business, sir?"

"Of course, ma'am, of course."

Anara's mind wandered while the Colonel prepared to share his battle plans. She knew such lack of attention did not suit her standing as commander of such a critical mission, but her thoughts refused to stay still.

"Is something wrong, Captain?" Fraser asked. "You seem preoccupied."

"I am sorry. There is a lot of work to be done. We left Earth in a bit of a hurry, as you are aware. We are space-worthy and we have enough supplies. Nevertheless, if we want to catch up with Jim's ship, I am going to have to push *Antariksh* to its limits. The second time in as many months. It is going to be rough."

"I understand...but are you sure there isn't anything else bothering you?" asked the Colonel, shrewdly.

Just the fact that I appreciate neither your mission nor your taking the place of Major Rawat. "No. There is nothing else. Let's start. I assume you want to discuss the plans for the capture of Jim's ship and possibly the capture of the TrueKif leadership back on KifrWyss?"

"You are correct. Kevin, will you bring up the plans for Operation Trikon?"

A holographic display appeared in the centre of the room filled with complex operational and technical data.

"I will not go too deep into the details right now, but we have multiple objectives. First, to identify, locate and bring the person or persons responsible for the Mumbai attack back to Earth to face trial. Second, to find and destroy any bases used by the TrueKif. The tertiary objective will be to rescue the KifrWyss leadership and the humans on HuZryss. Now, I will need your help in identifying and locating the leader of the TrueKif and their bases. We will definitely need help from the KifrWyss people opposing the TrueKif. What do you call them? The Discat?"

"That's right, the Discat. It is their form of government, somewhat like our own parliament. It's led by RyHiza," she told him. "But what makes you think Discat will help us?"

"I am afraid that is entirely in your domain, Captain. I am working under the assumption they will be willing to listen to the person who led the first contact mission."

"We have to see how that pans out," she remarked, non-commitally.

"Provided we can get the support, you and your team go in and bring them out. Is that it?' asked Ryan.

"It will not be quite so simple, Commander Ryan," replied Fraserl, stroking his chin. "As you know, military missions depend quite a bit on local intelligence for successful extraction. The layout of the land, strength of the opposition on the ground, their firepower—that sort of thing. As it stands, we have a very small chance of success if we go in blind."

He walked towards her. "Look, both of you have served in the armed forces of your respective countries. You know missions deep into enemy territory are always difficult. Mission Trikon is exactly like that. However, this is what we soldiers are trained for." His two subordinates nodded in unison.

"Our last trip to Alpha Centauri was quite eventful. It's a pity we did not have some the equipment we needed. I do hope you are well covered this time around?" asked Ryan. "I have seen your weapons manifest, but a lot of the stuff has been marked as classified."

"Yes, but there is no need for the classified status anymore. I will take you on a tour of the equipment personally. I assure you we are sufficiently prepared."

"Ok, I'll take your word for it," said Anara. "Commander Ryan can go over the details with you later."

"You yourself are not interested, Captain?"

Anara paused before answering. The primary objective for building *Antariksh* was no longer valid. "This was supposed to be ship of exploration, Colonel. That is what we set out to do when we started out on our journey almost two years ago. Since then, we have fought battles in space, discovered nuclear weapons hidden in secret compartments, been held hostage, and finally discovered that there are humans in another solar system, delivered there on the Voyager probe as human zygotes. Believe me when I say that I am not looking forward to another war."

Fraser gave her an appraising look. *She is thinking emotionally. Never a good sign during a military mission. Is this the only person they could find to command this ship? I had been told she is tough and capable, but all I can see is her vulnerability.*

"Better to be prepared to give the enemy a bloody nose, than fail in our mission. Indulge me for a while. Let me just show you what we have." He gestured with his hands, bringing up photos and details of the military equipment in the ship's cargo hold.

"Personal transporters—tracked, amphibious and flight capable," he said, scrolling through the list, "drones—armed and surveillance; light artillery, a few fixed-wing attack aircraft and of course, a full complement of commandos plus all the handheld weapons we will ever need, both laser and projectile. And a small complement of highly advanced robot soldiers."

"The JITF seems to be equipped like a small army," remarked Ryan.

"But we *are* a small army, Commander. I assure you this is by design and you will understand its necessity when we are on a strange planet, among a completely different species. We will have no backup, no extraction plans to a safe zone, and no one to call upon to help us. It is better to be prepared than to be caught off guard."

Anara knew he was right. She changed tack. "Why do we only have naval commandos?"

"Ahh. You see, the JITF is actually a multidisciplinary force of over a thousand men and women. We had very little time to prepare for this mission, but seeing as we are going to a planet inhabited by reptilians and possibly amphibious life, we thought it best to limit the team to people who can fight effectively in water and are equally deadly on land or in the air. Hence, the marine commandos form the bulk of this particular task force. Of course, we do have a complement of trained fighter pilots."

Anara studied the screen thoughtfully. "This does seem to be a lot of fire power, Colonel. I guess there is no escaping the fact that this is now a military operation and *Antariksh's* days of exploration are over. However, I do hope you will remember who is finally in charge—me. I will not allow us to go to war with a planet which is, for the most part, peaceful. Let's not forget they did raise our human children as foster parents."

"I expected you to take such a stand, Captain, but let me also state clearly; your prior military experience notwithstanding, the military operations will be under my direct command only. I will stay out of your way on the ship, and I request you stay out of my way on land."

Anara looked at him, considering his words. *He is right, of course. The PM said much the same thing. This is not a challenge to my authority. Just a simple submission of facts. It might complicate the situation when we are on KifrWyss and need to act quickly, but that's just another bridge to be crossed when we come to it. What is life, after all, if not the combination of opportunities, options and choices made?*

She decided against confronting the Colonel. This was neither the time nor the place for it. Besides, while she could handle diplomacy and flying a space ship, ground wars were another matter altogether.

She stood up, looked the Colonel in the eye for a long moment, then spun on her heel and left the room. Ryan looked surprise at this sudden turn of events, but followed her out dutifully. *What was she thinking?*

***

He caught up with her in the corridor. "What's your problem with him? Why are you being unnecessarily rude?"

"It's not about him, Ryan," said Anara, "I'm just not ready to replace Rawat so soon." Her shoulders drooped. "I know I am not being rational, but he represents everything that is wrong with this mission. He's ready for war, I'm not."

"It's not his fault. He is a soldier. He has a job to do, just like you. Please. Don't let your emotions overcome you. I am right here by your side. We will get through this together, all right?" He held her gently by her shoulders. She nodded.

But her mind was processing multiple thoughts at once. *Why can't I let go of the feeling that we are travelling to our doom?*

***

"Join you, Lieutenant?" Kevin was on a short break, and had been hoping quite fervently to run into Manisha. He was delighted to find her in the cafeteria.

"Oh. Of course, Major Kevin. Of course." She swallowed hurriedly, dabbed her mouth and moved her tray.

Kevin put his own tray down, and settled down on the chair beside her.

"So, Lieutenant, what do you do in your spare time when you're not flying this ginormous ship at the speed of light?"

"Ha!" she smiled. It was good opening line. "Let's see now. I read a lot. Crime thrillers, mostly. Do a bit of white hacking. Keeps me on my toes with computer systems, you know. And let's see, I do enjoy flying in simulators. You know, running a spaceship is not as easy as I make it sound." She smiled again. He thought it made her whole face light up. "What about you, Major Kevin?"

"Spear fishing, surfing, whenever I can get the time." He smiled back at her.

"That's so cool. I tried surfing once and spent most of my time in the water. I guess the sea and I are not meant for each other."

They lapsed into an awkward silence after that, each focusing on their tray and trying to come up with something interesting to say.

"Your captain came to meet the Colonel sometime back," Kevin said finally, breaking the silence. "They did not hit it off, that's for sure. She seems to be a capable skipper, but seems to not like having the JITF on board. Any idea what that's about?"

Manisha hesitated, unsure how much she could share with her new friend. She idolized Anara, but she had seen the changes in her in the time she had spent under her command.

"She's been under quite a lot of stress, you know. What with facing an attack when we met the aliens for the first time near Proxima Centauri—we barely escaped destruction—then finding that fertilised human eggs had been stored on Voyager 1 and the aliens had raised human children. Then the attack on Earth. She held the baby in her arms, Major, and talked Jim out of killing everyone in Mumbai and taking the child to HuZryss." She leaned a bit closer. "Don't tell anyone this but she had a run-in with Major Rawat in the beginning as well. She'll come around eventually. She has done more than can be asked of any spaceship captain, Major. I think she deserves a bit of slack. She's actually very warm and supportive to her people. Give her time." She patted his hand.

"Thanks for sharing that with me. I never meant to be disrespectful. Just curious. How about you taking up my offer for drinks?" Her hand was still on top of his.

5

The Second Ship

Anara lay still on her back on the floor of her cabin, arms at her side, palms facing upwards. The *savasana* pose generally helped her calm her mind, relax her body and get a good night's sleep. But even yoga had been failing her these past few weeks. Try as she might, she was not able to close her mind to the turmoil. The minute she closed her eyes, her demons returned to torment her. She hated being a pawn in this interstellar game of chess, tossed about from square to square.

She finally gave up, opened her eyes and sat up.

"Lights," she called out.

The room brightened. She looked about, glancing at the familiar objects that littered the shelves and the side table. Pictures of her parents, a water colour of Earth gifted by a school student before the first journey, an empty vase, and a few journals. A bright light shone briefly outside her porthole. She looked out of her window at the passing comet.

The ship had come out of *jump* a few hours ago. During the *jump* the ship travelled at faster-than-light speeds and the crew was confined to their sleeping capsules in the *dome.* The *dome* protected them from time dilation and relativistic effects while travelling at velocities that had been impossible to achieve till a couple of decades ago. The M-AM drive, gravity generators which bent space around the ship allowing it to break the light barrier, and the *dome* had allowed humankind to finally venture into deep space. During sub-light flight, standard protection systems built into the very structure of the ship functioned to keep the crew isolated, much like the heat shields on the ancient space shuttles of the twentieth century.

Due to the enormous power consumed during the *jump* the ship could travel at FTL speeds only for a few hours before it had to slow down and wait for the power plant to recharge. The recharging process itself took several hours, so the crew had a routine almost like a normal 9-to-5 working day.

Anara's thoughts had not become any clearer over the last few days and she worried she could be in the throes of a depression. Yet there was no one onboard she felt comfortable confiding in; not even the good doctor Khan. No, she decided, she had to deal with her demons herself. She needed to be fit if the crew was to succeed in their mission. *I can't let them down,* she reminded herself continually.

"Captain Anara to Ops, please," chimed Lieutenant Manisha's voice over the communication system.

Anara sighed deeply, acknowledged the request, and banished her worries to a deep corner of her mind. *How long before they surface again? I hope Manisha has something interesting to distract me. Duty calls.* She straightened her back, put on her shoes and walked out of the room.

***

She was not surprised to find Ryan in Ops. Lately he had been taking over more of her responsibilities and regular duties on board the ship. He knew something was troubling her but she was grateful that instead of intervening he had seemingly decided to give her the time and space to resolve her internal conflict.

"What's up, Commander?" she asked.

"Something really strange. Thought you should take a look. Hope I didn't disturb you?"

She waved away his concerns. "'Something' and 'strange' do not suit a vessel of exploration,

Commander." The words came out sounding harsher than she had intended.

"Sorry, Captain," Ryan replied somewhat self-consciously. "We have detected what looks like a ship during our routine scans."

"The TrueKif?" she queried, instantly alert.

"Does not seem so," Manisha interjected. "It is a design we are unfamiliar with. A few million kilometres ahead of us, travelling at sub-light velocity."

"Another alien ship?" asked Anara.

"Too far for us to make out right now," replied Ryan.

"Suggestions?"

"Recommend we increase speed or even perform a short, controlled *jump* to head them off and find out who they are and what they are up to," replied Ryan.

"Let's do it. Increase speed by 25%," Anara commanded.

They could not perceive the change, but the display climbed up to indicate a 25% increase in the ship's velocity. The distance between *Antariksh* and the strange ship closed slowly.

"We are making headway. It should be close enough for solid visuals in sixteen minutes," reported Manisha.

"Maintain this rate. Madhavan," she addressed her Chief of Engineering over the intercom, "any chance we can go faster?"

"I would not recommend that, Captain. Without the M-AM power, we are already over our top cruise velocity. I can hold this velocity for another couple of hours, but the engines are beginning to overheat."

"Noted. Keep me informed and maintain course and speed till further instructions."

The minutes passed slowly as the crew in Ops kept up their vigil.

"We are now two-and-a-half million kilometres out."

"Scan data. Go to aggressive gamma and x-ray scans." Anara had learnt some harsh lessons from their very first encounter with unknown ships in space. Don't hesitate, learn what you can, and don't give a damn if the other guy gets hurt in the process. She had her own ship to protect.

"Coming through. Spectroscopic analysis shows outer hull composed of poly-metallic alloys, fusion reactors—two of them. They seem to have some type of matter-anti matter drive technology. The ship is approximately fifty meters in length, and the hull composition and fusion reactants indicate..." She looked up in surprise. "The ship's from Earth."

"Copy that. Ryan?" This mission was getting too convoluted for her liking.

"Affirm. The metal composition is very similar to *Antariksh,* though somewhat more advanced. If I recall correctly this was the material proposed to be used in the construction of *Antariksh 2.* That ship is definitely from Earth," he stated confidently. "We are however, unable to penetrate inside."

"What a pretty set of mysteries we continue to run into, huh? Finding ships in the middle of nowhere, and each one presents a new surprise. No signs of the TrueKif ship, I assume?"

Manisha shook her head. "We've not seen any signs of them despite running scans."

"Any identifying signs on the hull of the ship?"

"Starting visual display now, ma'am." Manisha manipulated the long-range cameras. "There are some markings on the rear. Focusing."

The image became clearer.

"It's a flag. Searching database for a match."

"It's French," said Anara simply.

"Excuse me?" said Manisha.

"It's the flag of France. That means this is a French ship. Point is- what is a French ship doing in deep space? Last I checked *Antariksh* was the only ship capable of travelling outside the solar system, besides the older unmanned test ships. You know anything about this, Commander?"

"I'm as much in the dark as you are. What the hell are these guys doing out here?"

"Another secret mission?" Manish ventured. "Or maybe they're just lost?"

"We may never know that, Manisha, at least till we get closer or stop them. Are you sure the ship is moving under its own power and not adrift? Can we send them a signal or a message?"

"The ship's propulsion system is active. I am reading heat signatures from its engines. They are definitely not adrift. I will try signalling them now. Give me a minute," replied Ryan. A short while later he transmitted. *"Antariksh calling unknown vessel. Say again your call sign. Advise your intention. Antariksh calling unknown vessel."*

"Captain!" called out Manisha. "They are increasing speed and moving away from us. They're also changing direction. Looks like they've seen us too and are trying to avoid us."

"Why would they do that?" Anara wondered aloud. "They must have recognised us. This is the most famous ship in the entire solar system. They have to know we are allies." She turned to Ryan. "Is there anyone even on board or is it unmanned?" *Are they trying to escape? Do they have something to hide?*

"Unable to determine if it is manned. The ship is accelerating," Ryan reported.

"Try to keep up with them. Madhavan, I need more speed."

"I am giving you all we've got."

"Find some more, at least for a few minutes. We can't fall behind. I want to know why there is a French ship in this area and what they have to hide. Don't let them get away, Manisha. Keep an aggressive radar lock. C'mon Ryan, signal them again."

"Transmitting again. I am using standard Earth transmission frequencies. *Antariksh* to unknown vessel. Say again your call sign. Acknowledge." He listened for a minute. "No reply. No way they could have missed our signal. We're being ignored for sure."

***

On board the second ship, its captain sat at his console watching his radar readouts with concern. He had hoped to remain undetected for some more time. This encounter with *Antariksh* would unnecessarily complicate matters.

"*Capitaine*? We are receiving a transmission from the Indian ship. Do I respond?" called out his communications officer.

"*Ne fais rien,* Elise. Do nothing." *Damn that ship. Where did they come from? We were almost clear. I just need to avoid them for some more time. We have to find a way to escape the ship. How did the TrueKif ship vanish? This was the most direct route they could take on their way back to KifrWyss. We should have caught up with them. Where have Jim and his ship disappeared?*

***

"Still no response."

"Keep trying. Opinions? What do you think they are up to?"

Ryan sat still, staring at his screen. "Impossible to determine their purpose till we speak to them. We should keep in mind the possibility that this may be an unmanned vessel programmed not to interact with anyone." He swiped his fingers and posted the data onto the main display. "They are still ignoring us. Narada," he addressed the ship's AI, "take over the transmission. Repeat every five minutes. Report on response."

"Yes, Commander. Captain, do you want to call Colonel Fraser to Ops? This may turn into a tactical engagement," offered Narada.

"Not right now. We need to learn more. For the moment, just check out any data on the ship—origin, probable mission, anything you can find. And extrapolate based on their maximum possible speed when they might have launched from Earth. Get the data quickly."

"Roger. I will get back to you shortly."

Anara turned her attention back to Ryan. "An unmanned ship doesn't make sense, Ryan. This region has already been charted. All the data has been shared freely with other nations. There is nothing new to be learnt. It has to be a manned vessel. Question is—what are they after?"

Her query went unanswered as the pursuit continued.

"I have the preliminary details you had asked for, Captain," reported Narada.

"Shoot."

"The vessel design resembles the French vessel *Charles De Gaulle*. Its development was started a few years after construction began on *Antariksh*. Although very little information was made available, its design is believed to be FTL-capable. It was listed as a long-range exploration vessel with a crew complement of twenty-five. There is no known launch date for the *CDG*. Except for a few trial runs, it was not believed to be space-worthy yet. However, the vessel now in front of us seems to have been extensively modified from the original design. I have also calculated the most probable launch window which would put its position right here."

"And?" Ryan prompted.

"It was most likely launched within a window of plus-minus three days of our own."

"Why am I not surprised," said Anara, rolling her eyes. *No one tells me anything.* "Anything else?"

"It is possibly lightly armed with two laser cannons, and is likely to be led by Captain Antoine."

"Antoine? If this is the same Antoine who trained with me in 2105, then I know him well. A decent pilot, though a bit stubborn."

"Yeah. I remember him too," said Ryan. "Let's try this. Narada transmit the next message directly addressing Captain Antoine. Maybe that will get his attention."

The message went through – *"Captain Anara from spaceship Antariksh to Captain Antoine of unknown space vessel. Acknowledge. Caution. We will assume your intentions are hostile if you do not reply."*

***

"There is a message for you, *Capitaine.*"

"*Que voulez-vous dire*? What do you mean, for me?"

"It is addressed to you, *Capitaine Antoine. Dès Capitaine Anara."* reported Elise. *They seemed to know everything!*

"*Zutalors!* I will end this. Put me on."

***

This time there was a response. An image appeared on the holographic display.

"Hello, Captain Anara. It seems you have caught up with me." Antoine tried to keep a straight face. He had to throw them off his track, not share information.

"Hello, Commander, or is it Captain Antoine now? Looks like you finally got your own ship," said Anara looking at a familiar face though somewhat haggard. His face betrayed the fact that he was hiding something.

"Yes. A fine ship, no? But I am sure you did not call to chit chat."

"It did seem strange finding you this deep in space. Would you be willing to share what exactly you and your ship are doing here?"

"No, I would not share our purpose with you. Niceties over, Captain. Stay out of our way if you value your safety!"

***

"End contact. Do not accept any more transmissions, Elise! *Sous-entendu?* Understood?"

***

The holo image on *Antariksh* blinked off leaving behind a stunned silence in Ops.

6

Intricacies

"Well, that was quite rude, don't you think?" drawled a voice from the door, and the tall figure of Colonel Fraser entered the room.

Anara ignored his remark.

"Why are they here? A secret mission?" asked Manisha.

"There is only one mission that I can think of, Manisha. They are after the TrueKif ship." Anara chewed her lip thoughtfully. "The PM said we're out of the group of 8. I don't know if we've managed to make our way back into the group yet, even if they did support the mission with JITF. It is likely the French are out too. With the collaboration gone, they might be looking to steal any advantage they can. Point is, even if FTL-capable, that small ship cannot hope to reach the Alpha Centauri system. Then, the TrueKif ship seems to be the most likely target, no?"

Ryan was thinking along the same lines. "I agree. It is unlikely they would be looking to capture the aliens, because their vessel will not be a match for the alien ship in a fight. This has to be a rogue mission by the French, or someone else, to... I don't know; seize the technology aboard the TrueKif ship?"

Anara nodded. "Captain Antoine is ready to use deadly force to protect his interests. He openly threatened to attack us. It can only mean one thing—they are after the bomb, the device which Jim was carrying. This is not good. We need to stop them."

Fraser pitched in. "Sounds like a lot of speculation to me. But like you said, we can't learn anything till we force them to reveal their secrets. Military strategy would suggest that we fire a warning shot and show them that we are serious. And if that fails to stop them then we fire again – only this time we try and disable their ship."

"I am well aware of that strategy, Colonel Fraser," Anara retorted testily, "but I am unwilling to escalate things on the basis of speculation. We will shoot if required, but only after I have confirmation of their true purpose. We will track them for now and wait for another opportunity. Keep following them, Manisha.

Ryan, compose a message to Earth and transmit. Share everything we have observed so far." Signals could only travel at the speed of light since humans had not yet mastered the acceleration of radio signals beyond that speed over large distances. She did not expect a reply, but she had to check in with Indian Space Command back on Earth and pass on the information.

"Yes ma'am, I will keep us on their trail, but it will be difficult if the *Charles De Gaulle* jumps to FTL. We will never be able to locate them again if that happens," replied Manisha.

Ryan thought for a moment. "That may be so, but I'm sure they can only *jump* in straight lines just like us, we need to be prepared to *jump* right after them on a pursuit course. Besides they need to recharge too. I think we can keep up." He reached a conclusion and shared it. "Look, the TrueKifs were headed back to KifrWyss. That is also our destination and, no doubt, that of the *CDG* as well. We just need to follow our original course and it will keep us on their tail. Stay sharp and keep up as far as possible," said Ryan. "Narada, keep plotting their course changes. Inform the crew to be prepared for a *jump* at a moment's notice."

"Of course, Commander," acknowledged Narada.

"You okay with this, Captain?" Ryan turned and asked Anara for confirmation.

"Yes. Yes. Of course. Go ahead." Anara was getting distracted again. *Who can I trust if even our allies are not above such scheming?*

"Are you seriously planning to play safe here?" demanded Fraser.

"Yes I am, Colonel. This party is still under my command." Her reply was curt.

"And what if the *CDG* moves on a trajectory which takes us away from our destination? What then?" Fraser was persistent.

That was a real possibility. "Let's not get ahead of ourselves here. We wait and watch," Anara said, with finality.

The crew watched the exchange in uncomfortable silence, most of them pretending to carry on their real or imaginary tasks.

"You have control, Commander. I will be available if required." Without another glance at the Colonel, Anara walked out.

"That lady is carrying a rather large chip on her shoulder, isn't she?" Fraser muttered to Ryan.

"I'm sure she has a lot on her mind and, as it so happens, I agree with her approach," Ryan responded, and was pleased to see that his reply had left the Colonel confused.

"Ok, people. You have your orders. Don't let the ship out of our sight." Ryan opened the ship-wide communications. "This is Commander Ryan. We are currently pursuing a vessel of Earth origin. It may turn out to be hostile. All personnel to continuously staff their stations in rotating shifts unless otherwise instructed. Be prepared for an emergency *jump*. You will have forty-five seconds to get to the *jump* capsules when indicated. Ryan out."

***

Manisha finished her shift and made her way to the senior crew lounge. It had become more and more difficult to get a few minutes of peace and quiet in the midst of all the recent events. She hoped the Major would also be able to make the rendezvous.

She smiled when she entered the lounge and saw him sitting in an easy chair. He was facing the porthole, away from her, with a half-empty glass in his hand. She liked spending her free time in the lounge, which, though rather small, had soft lighting, a small library of books and reading devices and, of course, an outstanding music system.

"I didn't know you were fond of classical music, Major?"

Kevin rose and turned with a smile on his face. "I've never spent so much time in deep space. The view is so mesmerizing. I can spend hours just sitting here gazing out of the window. The music? Now that was already playing when I reached here. It seemed appropriate. How're you doing, Lieutenant or can I call you Manisha?"

"Pretty good, sir, and Manisha is fine. This new development is something else, isn't it? I assume you have been briefed?"

"Of course. You guys seem to have a penchant for finding random enemy ships in space." His soft laugh was attractive. "And no need to call me 'sir'. We are from completely different services. Last I checked, ISC was a civilian organisation. Kevin will do just fine."

Manisha nodded, turned to pick up a soft drink from the sideboard and settled herself down next to Kevin for a few minutes of small talk that she was sure she was going to enjoy.

***

Anara sat at the edge of her bed, her palms pushing down on the mattress. She had turned off the lights. The room was dark. Her eyes closed, she forced herself to breathe slowly and calm down. She was furious at herself for having lost control and snapped at the Colonel. His query has been quite reasonable, if not his tone. By turning it into a confrontation she had displayed behaviour unbecoming of her position.

What is happening to me? How did I get like this this way? Is it only the loss of Major Rawat or the fact that we narrowly avoided a huge tragedy back in Mumbai or have I become disillusioned with the powers that be? Tej did everything in her power to arrest me. Then the PM manipulated me. Is this how people react when faced with extreme danger? Am I becoming like them? Why am I lashing out at the Colonel? No. This is not me. I can't allow my stress to change who I am. Yes, I went against my beliefs and accepted nuclear weapons on my ship. Yes, I allowed the PM to browbeat me. But I can't let my crew down. I can do this. This is my ship and my mission.

7

An Enemy Unseen

For the next several hours, *Antariksh* engaged in an elaborate game of cat and mouse with the *CDG*, even as the crew kept an eye open for the TrueKif ship. The nimbler *Charles De Gaulle* tried any number of strategies to escape but the larger and more powerful *Antariksh* managed to keep up every time. Multiple short *jumps* saw the crew rushing repeatedly to the *dome*. However, Ryan and Manisha expertly countered every move of the *CDG*. They were still hot on the tail of the French ship.

Anara was conspicuously absent from Ops during that time, locked away in her room. Deducing correctly that she needed time to pull herself together, Ryan had decided to leave her alone. He was confident of handling this hunt on his own and knew Anara would return to her usual, efficient self eventually. She had placed her trust in him to keep the operations running, and so far, Ryan had managed to keep both the crew and the ship working at peak efficiency.

Anara finally appeared in Ops two days after their first encounter with the other vessel. She smiled when she entered the doorway and Ryan was visibly relieved to see her. Fresh and brimming with newfound confidence, she seemed to have suppressed her demons for now.

She went and stood right in the centre of the room, legs akimbo, hands crossed behind the back and an intense look on her face as she concentrated on the holographic display.

"Ryan, it has been two days since we started this chase. They must know by now that they don't have a chance in hell of getting away from us."

Ryan agreed. "If I were in their position, my only hope of escape would be to locate the TrueKif ship and somehow take control of it in the few hours before *Antariksh* caught up."

"Right. So, he must be searching really hard for the ship, correct?"

"Yes, and so are we. Narada has been running simulations and all manners of scans to locate Jim's ship. Unfortunately, he has not been successful yet."

"Then why don't we stop being the followers and take the lead?"

"Lead? You mean by leapfrogging ahead of them?"

She nodded, a sly gleam in her eyes. "We get the Easter egg first. Deny them the prize they seek so desperately. Then maybe they'll talk."

"Got it, Captain. Manisha, let's prepare for an extended *jump*." He felt relieved. After the long passive chase, it was good to take proactive action. Plot a fifteen-minute *jump* cycle at maximum velocity on our original course. That should get us at least six hours ahead of the *CDG*. Madhavan, time to show us what your ship can do," he barked over the intercom.

"Affirm, but you're gonna run this ship into the ground with your hide-and- seek, Commander. When is it going to end?"

"Patience, Mr Madhavan, patience. Ready, Manisha?"

"Three minutes to *jump* cycle. Countdown starting now," confirmed Manisha from her station. "All posts secured."

"Good. Get the crew moving."

Ops started emptying out as the non-essential personnel left for the *dome*. Manisha and Anara would remain in the Ops cocoon for the *jump*.

"All green for the jump. Ready to execute on your command," reported Narada. Manisha and Anara had settled into the miniature *dome* in Ops.

"Execute," commanded Anara.

The M-AM engines engaged and *Antariksh* accelerated. As it crossed the speed of light the space outside darkened and then went black. The portholes transformed into virtual screens to show normal space. It was going to be a short *jump* and Manisha kept a sharp eye to ensure that they stopped at the terminus she'd plotted, well ahead of the French ship.

The lack of external data inputs during the *jump* had always rankled Anara. They were effectively blind while the ship flew at FTL. The straight-line course was plotted before the *jump* and could be terminated in an emergency, like if they encountered a solid object in their path, but they depended on the pre-flight scans of the flight path to avoid any collisions. Interstellar dust and minor objects would not be detected, but the front shielding could handle those. However, a large object impacting the ship at FTL speeds would drill a large hole in its body, possibly destroying it. To counter this threat, the outermost layer of the four-layer shield consisted of a laser array, which sent out continuous rays of high intensity beams that blasted away any large particles that came in the ship's path well in advance. The second layer was a magnetic screen to repel smaller space dust and other particles. Larger non-magnetic objects would bounce off the secondary shield in the third layer which physically projected out a few meters in front of the bow. It was meant to operate like a shield to absorb the impact of and deflect small foreign objects. Finally, the outermost part of the hull consisted of multi-layered composites, which could automatically regenerate if damaged. Even so, the flight path was carefully plotted in advance to circumvent large obstacles.

"Five... four... three... two... one. And we have reached the terminus, Captain," Manisha said, as the M-AM powered down.

Anara unbuckled herself and waited for the *dome* in Ops to power down, then she walked over to the centre of the room.

"Narada, activate the main display." The AI complied.

"What the hell? Narada, why is the display convoluted? All I can see is a distorted image. It looks like a fish-eye."

"Yes. Adjusting display."

"Well?" demanded Anara when the image did not clear up.

"No effect. The holographic and imaging cameras are working flawlessly. The space outside seems to be distorted."

"What do you mean 'distorted'? How can space be distorted? Analyse and clarify?" Anara was annoyed. They were losing precious time. *Had something gone wrong during the jump?*

"A minute to analyse please?" There was a short pause. "Okay, Captain, the display if working optimally. The image we can see is a real time presentation of the space outside. The space *is* distorted. Something is affecting light and objects within visible distance."

"Possible causes?"

"My findings indicate there are three possible causes—one, an object is blocking our sensors. To do that it would have to be extremely large in size. Two, a transient interstellar object of unknown origin, like a large comet is warping our signals and causing a distortion. Or three, there is a black hole which is absorbing all light energy and matter in the region including our energy beams and possibly causing gravitational lensing, making us see the stars behind it."

"Black hole, huh? Nah, that's too farfetched," said Anara dismissively. "Tell me, was this phenomenon present during our last flight?"

"No. Such an intriguing phenomenon could not have been missed. It would have been charted and would show up on our updated maps."

"Yeah. But how did you miss it in the pre-*jump* scans?

"I did miss it," he admitted. "My programming works on standard navigational criteria which include a large number of parameters. Unfortunately, a phenomenon such as this is not part of standard criteria."

"Hmm. We will need to start including non-standard phenomenon specifications from now onwards. I'll get someone to work on it. Anyway, each of the possibilities you have named are highly unlikely. A scanning beam would have detected a large object. Also, I have never heard of a comet this large in size. And black holes don't just appear out of thin air, do they now?"

Manisha was listening quietly to this exchange. "Should I gather the senior officers, and sound an alert?"

"No alerts. But yes, get Ryan and others up here immediately."

Manisha sent out the call for the officers to assemble in Ops.

Narada waited to get Anara's attention before he spoke again. "Captain, I agree the options seem unlikely. A black hole would require a star which is at least twenty times as massive as our own sun to collapse under its own gravity. There are other predicted models for the formation of black holes including extremely high-energy collisions of great density, or the conditions created inside a particle accelerator used by experimental physicists. The Extreme Graviton Collider on the moon has created several such singularities which have lasted long enough to be studied."

"Narada, Narada," said Anara, shaking her head, not buying into his arguments. "We don't have a particle accelerator anywhere nearby and the high energy particles created in a lab would not exist in space on their own violation. Such particles would need temperatures in the range of millions of degrees to get that kind of energy."

"You are right about that. Such temperatures exist at the core of the Sun or in our own matter-antimatter reaction chambers only."

"Say again. What?" Ryan had just entered the room.

"At the core..."

"No need, Narada. It was a rhetorical question. What's going on, Captain?"

Anara quickly brought Ryan up to speed.

Ryan listened carefully, while he looked over the available data on his screen and entered some commands.

Anara watched him saying nothing. Ryan was a theoretical physicist by training, and if anyone could figure this out it would be him.

Leaving him at his work, she sidled over to Manisha. "Dig up some data on black holes, will you?"

"Of course, ma'am," Manisha replied and entered the relevant commands. Her screen displayed copious amounts of text and she started reading it out aloud. "Black holes are singularities," she read, "characterized by an intense gravity field which does not allow anything to escape its attraction, not even light. Though theorised since the beginning of the twentieth century, no black hole has ever been closely observed in the last two hundred years, though there are quite a few photographs taken by deep space radio telescopes, including that of the supermassive black hole at the centre of our own galaxy." Manisha looked up. "I remember all the photographs developed using radio telescopes, but they were only able to capture images of black holes with accretion discs."

Anara nodded, and she continued, "Black holes are formed when a sufficiently compact mass deforms spacetime. Generally, such compact masses are formed after the collapse of a very massive star possibly after a supernova explosion of said star."

"That is high school physics. As is the fact that they cannot be detected directly since electromagnetic radiation cannot escape their gravitational pull. We can only observe their presence through their interaction with interstellar materials, like when they absorb other stars or planets. They can also be observed indirectly by measuring changes in gravitational waves, or their interaction with light. They will bend light from sources behind them in a phenomenon known as gravitational lensing."

Anara looked over, then walked across to Ryan's station. "We have no missing stars near Earth certainly not within four light years. In fact, there are no stars within that distance, certainly not something twenty times as big as our sun. This phenomenon is not a black hole," observed Anara, pursing her lips. "We are looking at something which should not even be here in this region of space."

Ryan nodded. "Give me a few minutes, please? I will confirm our findings. Jas," he called out to another crewmember as she entered Ops, "run some simulations. I'm sending across the parameters." He looked down as his back screen and worked silently, unintentionally ignoring Anara.

She turned back to Manisha "Get working with Narada. Get me information on the other possibilities while we wait for Ryan to finish his research."

"Do you think this is serious enough to merit this much attention? We might miss the *CDG* if we get distracted."

"Manisha, in my many years of flying in space, I have never seen a phenomenon such as this. Never. The *CDG* is no longer our top priority. We need to understand if this poses any threat to *Antariksh* and its crew before we go any further. If our *jump* went as programmed, we are way ahead of the *CDG*, anyway. So, let's not worry about them for now. This is more important. Proceed as directed." Anara turned back and stood staring at the holo-image, her eyes searching for clues, as she waited for her team to find her some explanations. *I need to be patient.*

8

Event Horizon

Anara fidgeted in her seat. It had been quite some time since Ryan had immersed himself in finding answers to the latest puzzle facing them.

The dark mass was now in the dead centre of the holographic display as Antariksh continued on its course. Anara's sixth sense was tingling away but she did not have sufficient information to take a decision yet. Whatever was out there was not a normal occurrence. She needed answers from Ryan, however half-baked they may be.

"Ryan," she called out. He ignored her. She raised her voice and called him again, "Ryan?"

He finally looked up, acknowledging her.

"Do you have anything to share? We can't just wait around while you pretend you're studying as if you're back in university."

Ryan smiled at her sarcasm. He rubbed his eyes and ran a hand through his dark blond hair. Astonishingly, his hair was all in one place. No signs of stress there. How she envied his silky locks.

"The sarcasm is unbecoming of you, Captain, and actually, yes, I was enjoying myself. I apologise. I heard what Manisha was telling you about black holes. But I think there is more."

He got up from his seat and stretched, then walking over to the centre of the room, he clasped his hands behind his back and paced around trying to gather his thoughts. He was deliberately being slow. He need time to process his findings. The conclusion was too fantastic.

"You are absolutely correct when you said that black holes cannot be seen. They are perfect black bodies, objects that absorb all radiation and reflect no light back. And as you're aware if an object does not reflect or radiate light, it cannot be seen and remains invisible. But I'm getting ahead of myself." He continued, "I have run multiple scans of the phenomenon and have been unable to get any readings of any type about the object. I have to conclude that it is absorbing all electromagnetic radiation directed at it including those from our sensor beams. As I said earlier a normal object would have reacted differently. Also, any sufficiently large object has enough gravity to exhibit a lensing effect, I mean the refraction of light from other sources such as stars behind it. I have been able to determine some such lensing around the central area of this thing in front of us. Light from the stars behind it is being bent causing the minutest of lensing."

He paused as the door opened and Colonel Fraser entered Ops. He came and stood on Captain Anara's side but her eyes remained focussed on Ryan. There was something big coming up. *Now what?*

"I proceeded on the assumption," Ryan went on, "that this is a black hole. That is a logical conclusion in view of all the available evidence." He glanced around the group as if expecting someone to challenge him. When no one commented he picked up his discourse again. "We will run a few tests shortly to check our assumptions and I hope we are on time, but it may already be too late. The die may have already been cast even before the Captain noticed the object."

"Event horizon!" breathed Anara.

"Yes, I believe we are already inside it."

"But, how could we not have noticed it? What about the accretion disc or gravitational effects?"

Anara strode over to him and they continued debating the physics.

Fraser found their discussion incomprehensible. He turned to a crewmember sitting at a nearby station. "So, what's going on here?"

"We seem to have encountered an unknown phenomenon, Colonel," crewmember Jas responded. "They are trying to understand it better."

"What phenomenon? Why is there a fish-eye on the holo display?"

"It's a black hole, or what we believe is a black hole"

"Black hole? But those have those bright golden shiny discs around them, no? What do you call them?"

"Accretion discs. Intense circles of light and matter," Jas explained. "But those would only be present around black holes of a certain size which have swallowed a star or several planet-size bodies. The energetic particles from the absorbed matter may stay just at the edge of the event horizon, forever caught in a no man's land, or slowly entering the core of the black hole. What we have in front of us may be a black hole that just does not have sufficient mass or has not sucked in enough matter to form an accretion disc. And Colonel, they believe we may be caught within the event horizon."

"That is the boundary of the black hole, right? From which nothing can escape? But wouldn't we know if we entered that boundary?" asked Fraser.

"No, Colonel. You must understand no one has ever entered any event horizon before; there is no way to know when you enter it... it's impossible to map."

"You sure we are inside the event horizon?"

Jas shrugged. "That's nor for me to say, sir." Fraser looked over to Ryan and Anara.

"I should have acted sooner," Anara was saying.

"I wouldn't blame you for this, Captain," Ryan said. "There was no way you could have known about this. There is no way anyone could have known about this. Even now, till we observe the phenomenon up close, I'd not bet on me being right." Anara had this bad habit of taking personal responsibility for everything that went wrong. It could be mentally crippling. He was learning to offer his support as soon as she exhibited such behaviour. He looked her in the eyes and offered reassurance. She nodded ever so slightly.

"Manisha, all stop. We will not go any further till we have more information. Send a message to the *CDG* warning them of the threat ahead. We don't know where they are, and the signal may not reach them, but we owe them that much."

"All stop, ma'am. Message transmitted," Manisha acknowledged.

Within a few moments Manisha looked up in surprise, her eyes worried. "Captain, the engines have stopped but we are still moving forward. Mr. Madhavan, are you reading this?" Her voice jolted Madhavan in the engine room.

"How can that be?" came the surprised voice of Madhavan over the intercom. He rapidly crossed the room and bent at his station to check the engine status for himself. "She's right, Captain. Engines are stopped but we still have forward movement."

"This is what you were referring to, weren't you Ryan?"

He nodded. "We are caught into the gravity well. I was right. Madhavan," he called over the intercom, "reverse all engines now. We might just be able to break free if we can punch out enough juice."

"Nothing exits the event horizon, Ryan," Anara said in a whisper.

"Yes, but this black hole may not yet have gravity strong enough to hold us. Do you want to give up without a fight? Perhaps, if we can achieve FTL speeds... we have to try!"

She nodded.

Everyone felt the vibrations of the engines as they built up power, working against the pull of gravity.

"Power levels at 25% reverse. Forward movement has not slowed," Manisha's voice was calm but the minute beads of sweat on her forehead told a different story.

"Noted," Anara said. "Increase power in increments of 25%. One minute's dwell at each stage to observe."

"Yes, ma'am, increasing to 50%."

With each increment in the engines' output, hull vibrations increased exponentially as *Antariksh* struggled to break free. The engines were now at a hundred percent of rated power and still the ship refused to move. The crew could almost feel the inexorable pull of the black hole's gravitational power. Even the formidable power that *Antariksh* could work up was clearly not enough to save it. The ship refused to move in reverse.

"Cross over into red zone," Anara snapped. "My authorisation. Increase power to 120%." She could not allow the others to feel the fear inside her. She moved slightly to the right, stood behind her chair and put both her hands on its back. She needed the support. Her fingers dug deep into the soft fabric.

Antariksh almost jumped as the power output on the display touched 120. For a split second it appeared like a miracle may happen. But the small reverse motion ceased almost immediately, and the ship moved inexorably forward again although a little slower than earlier.

"Do you have anything more to give me, Madhavan?" Anara called out over the intercom.

"I can barely hold the engines at this level. We are going to tear apart. Hull stress is at 160% of safety limits. You've got to dial back!" He just had snatches of conversation to go on, but his own station was displaying a copy of the holo-image from Ops. He knew what Ryan was talking about and wanted to escape as much as the next person, but he knew that *Antariksh* would not be able to stand the strain for more than a few minutes. He did not want to tear the ship apart and die in open space.

Ominous creaks sounded around Ops and the room was bathed in crimson hues from innumerable warning lights from every console.

All eyes turned to Anara as she stood still, gripping the back of her chair, almost as if she were trying to hold *Antariksh* back through sheer willpower alone. Her black eyes were fixated on the holo display as if daring the black hole to challenge her authority over the ship.

"Captain!" shouted Ryan, breaking through her concentration. "We can't hold this any longer. We have to stop!"

She nodded imperceptibly. Just a small motion of her head. Ryan confirmed her order to Madhavan.

Round 1 to the black hole, if that is what it was. It helped to objectify the black hole as an enemy. As always with Anara, once the enemy was known, her path became clearer. Her concentration was absolute, and her resolve hardened. This was not yet over. *I will prevail*

"That did not work. We are definitely within the event horizon." Ryan looked out the window. There was a strange glow streaming in from the front of the ship. He turned around. There was deep blackness outside the porthole to the rear of the ship. *What now? Extreme red-shifting, or something else?*

"Absolutely sure?"

"Look outside the portholes. All light is being pulled in towards the centre of the hole. The same light is travelling away from us. The space behind us is bright while in front towards the black hole it is dark. That's not a good sign. I don't have enough data but if this is a Schwarzschild-type singularity then there will be no escape for us. However, if we are lucky and this is a charged, or rotating, or Kerr type of black hole, we might yet have a chance. But whatever we want to try will have to be done fast. Very fast." He cursed inwardly in having wasted precious time in resolving the data. But there was nothing else he could have done. At least now, he could bring forth a sense of urgency.

"Each of those types of black holes have completely different characteristics, Ryan. All we have to go on are theoretical models of black holes. How do we make sure which one this is?"

"I don't know enough about it yet to make a judgment call. All I can determine is that by looking at our lack of success so far, we cannot escape by using the power we have employed so far."

"Care to explain that in plain English, Commander?" asked the Colonel. So far, he had been standing quietly near Jas, observing the action. A trained soldier, he knew when he was out of his depth. There would be many more such instances during the journey, he was sure of that. *Maybe it was time for him to brush up on physics as well.*

"Sorry, Colonel. Not right now. Ryan and I have work to do." Anara was curt but not rude this time. She pulled up a chair and got busy with Ryan trying to solve equations that had puzzled the best brains in physics over many centuries. She did have something none of the physicists before could ever dream off—solid experimental data right there in front of her.

"Here, sir. I'll try and explain," said Jas. "We really may not have time to get into all the details, though." She closed her fist, made a pulling motion, using gestures to pull up a virtual screen, and drew a small circle in the centre of the screen with her forefinger. "Assume this is a singularity, Colonel, okay?"

"Uh, pardon my ignorance but what is a singularity?"

"It's a region where spacetime curvature cannot be measured. It's infinite."

Fraser raised his eyebrows. Jas looked at screen to see if her black hole gravity simulation was still running. She decided that she did have a couple of minutes to spare and sighed, thinking uncharitably that he had better dumb down his explanation even further for the present audience.

"A singularity is a point where all matter is compressed into zero volume and therefore has infinite density, see? We know that all matter exerts a gravitational force on all other matter in the universe. The larger the mass, the stronger is its gravitational pull. Gravity at the surface of our sun is around twenty-eight times more than that on Earth while, gravity on the moon is one-sixth that of Earth since it is that much smaller. The effect of gravity also reduces when distance increases but that is not relevant right now. Now, a black hole singularity has a gravitational force thousands of times stronger than that of our sun depending on the amount of mass it has swallowed up.

It is so strong that even photons of light moving at a velocity of 300000 km/sec cannot escape."

She drew a large circle around the smaller circle. "This larger circle represents what is known as the event horizon, the boundary from within which light cannot escape from the gravity of the singularity. This is the point of no return. The boundary can be very large. Did you know that gravity is the weakest of all physical forces, but it can act over extremely large distances even thousands of light years?"

"And you are saying that we are inside this event horizon?"

"In all likelihood, yes we are. And as you have observed we cannot escape. We are trapped."

"But shouldn't the extreme gravity here be affecting us already?" Fraser struggled to find the exact word he had heard earlier. "Something about stretching into spaghetti! Yes, spaghetti?"

"You mean spaghettification? The ship has built-in protection systems besides the *dome* which keep us safe from the effects of time dilation and gravity even when we are flying slower than the speed of light. I believe, gravity will overcome our systems as we get closer to the centre, but we should be safe for some time."

"So, what happens now?" Fraser asked, louder than he had intended.

"What happens, Colonel," Anara said, "is that we get pulled into the centre of the black hole, into the singularity, and then we die."

9

Battle Against Gravity

The crew in Ops looked at one another in shock. The reality of the situation was finally sinking in. Ryan glared at his drawing on the virtual screen as if he expected it to provide a solution. Once more he cursed inwardly. The years spent studying physics would not be of much help today. He knew about black holes, he had learnt even more in the past hour possibly more than any other human because he had managed to study one from such close proximity. Yet his knowledge was miniscule. Three hundred years had passed since black holes had first been theorised and humankind was still not prepared to deal with one of them in its own backyard. At least *Antariksh* now had the dubious distinction of being the first earth ship to reach a singularity. First ship to fly FTL in interstellar space. First to meet aliens. First to find a black hole. These were enough achievements for a lifetime.

"Well, technically, that is not correct," he said, just to break the eerie silence in Ops. "We will not die so soon. We will be pulled towards the singularity, stretched into strands due the difference in gravity and then crushed into nothingness. We will become part of an enormously large, compact mass of matter. Yes, we will die but our quantum information may yet be preserved and who knows, maybe it will live forever. In essence, if not in life, we will be alive."

"Really, Ryan? And how is that any better?"

"Sorry. I just thought if we are to die we might as well die with an attitude!"

Anara shook her head in exasperation at this, then turned to face the rest of her crew. "I did not intend to sound quite so dramatic, folks, but it's better we face the reality of our situation. We will need to work together if we are to succeed. Time is short, right Ryan?"

"Umm, we may actually have a lot more time at hand than you think."

"How so?"

"Time dilation. As we reached nearer the event horizon, if there is a ship outside watching us, it will see us go in very very slowly. Of course," said Ryan, realising he was wrong even as he was speaking, "for us nothing would change. Our time would flow linearly at the same rate. Sorry, right theory, wrong conclusion."

"Yeah. Good for the rest of the universe. They can watch us die in slow motion," said Anara drily.

The Colonel was as shaken as anyone else in the room. What a spectacular way to meet death! But he kept quiet. He walked in a few more steps, his uniform crisp and creased, his boots silent against the carpet on the floor.

"What do you intend to do now?" he asked. "Give up and wait to become history?"

"Not on your life. We will fight to the bitter end. We have still not put out all the power at our disposal or our fastest speed.

"We should go to FTL, yes?" Ryan asked, reading her mind. "It might work." His blue eyes met hers and a look was exchanged. It was a very long shot, but they had to try for the sake of the hundred lives under their command.

"Agreed. Narada," she addressed the AI. "Emergency *jump* protocols. Sixty seconds countdown. Everyone, out of Ops and into the *dome.* Sound the alarm to alert the crew."

The klaxon came to life and the red revolving lights galvanized the crew into action. There was a rush for the exit, then their training took over and a controlled mass moved to prepare for the emergency *jump* cycle. A disembodied voice continued the countdown and alarm in the background.

"Narada, you have autonomous control," Anara confirmed as she and Ryan entered the mini-dome in Ops and strapped themselves in.

"Twenty seconds to *jump*. Crew is accounted for," confirmed Narada.

"Do you believe in God, Ryan?" she asked.

"I do now, and believe me I am praying as hard as I can."

Five... four... three... two... one...

They barely felt the initial force as the FTL system was engaged.

"We are moving, Captain," Narada reported a few seconds later and their display confirmed the information. "Velocity is one hundred kilometres per second."

"That's all?" mouthed Ryan at Anara. "It's not working out."

"Give it a few minutes. Let's wait and see."

"Velocity rising to two hundred kilometres per second." A few more seconds passed. "Correction - velocity now at 90 kilometres per second and dropping."

"Bring all engines online, Narada. Increase reactor output to 120%."

"That is not recommended, ma'am. At 120% if we do not break free in twenty seconds, the ship's hull will disintegrate."

"Just do it. We will use every precious second that we have."

"Acknowledged. Output now at 120% of maximum. Hull stress at 175% of safety factor."

"Ten seconds, stress at 200% and rising. Fifteen seconds to break up. Velocity down to twenty kilometres per second. You must disengage! Disengage now!"

"All right. All right. Disengage all engines," she commanded.

Their gambit had failed.

10

Theories And Speculations

With the *jump* aborted mid-way, the crew slowly trickled back into Ops. News had spread rapidly throughout the ship. *Antariksh was trapped. They could not escape. Death was near.* Yet the crew acted with equanimity, concentrating on their tasks, keeping their heads down, praying silently for another chance to see their families.

"What do we do now?" asked Manisha tentatively.

Anara paced the centre of Ops, her brows tightly knit, her face clouded with a mixture of anger and frustration. She was still hiding her emotions from the crew. More than a hundred lives depended on her and she had no fresh ideas to counter the 'enemy'. Aliens, interstellar travel, nuclear bombs—she'd managed them all only to be finally defeated by a force of nature which was barely understood. But she could not let her team down. Not now. Not ever.

"I'm not certain, Lieutenant," she replied with a calmness belying the turmoil in her mind. She stopped pacing and stood in front of the central holographic display. "Where's the French ship? Do we know?" she asked no one in particular, then looked around with questioning eyes when nobody answered. She ran a hand through her decidedly unkempt hair. There had been no time for personal grooming or rest over the past several hours. She was tired, mentally rather than physically. Taking a handful of her shoulder-length hair, she tied it up in a rough bun. "Ryan?"

"We lost track of them a couple of hours ago. The instruments are going crazy. We're not getting any returns on our scans. Every electromagnetic or particle signal we send out seems to be getting sucked right into the black hole."

"And if light cannot escape then neither can we." It was an oft-repeated statement that day. Ryan nodded in confirmation.

Anara looked around at the people surrounding her. A couple of them were standing, but most of them were slouched down in their seats.

"Maybe we will have better luck if we can understand this bloody phenomenon, don't you think?" the Colonel spoke up. "I, for one, am still somewhat lost with whatever is going on here."

"Ryan and I checked out the possibilities. There really is not much to go on. With *Antariksh* caught within the event horizon, our data gathering has gone almost to zero. We can see behind us in a manner of speaking, but we cannot see anything in front. But maybe thinking out aloud may help sharpen our choices. You want to explain to the Colonel, Ryan?"

"I have a question too. If you are correct and this is really a black hole, then why is no accretion disc visible?" asked Manisha.

For the briefest moment, Fraser congratulated himself – he knew something that Manisha did not. All thanks to Jas.

Ryan pushed himself up from the table he had been leaning against and pulled up a diagram of a dot at the centre of a circle on the virtual display, quite similar to the one drawn by Jas for the Colonel.

"We know about the singularity at the centre of a black hole and its event horizon, right? Basically, there is infinite density at the singularity because all matter is compressed into zero volume and gravity is immense causing all matter and energy to be sucked right in. As the black hole grows and sucks in more and more matter, its gravitational pull increases. The matter being sucked in—some of this matter heats up as it nears the black hole, but not all of it enters the event horizon. Some of it remains at the edge of the horizon, heating up as the particles collide with each other at extremely high speeds. This forms a swirling ring of heated matter and light, which scientists refer to as an accretion disc."

With his fingers, he drew a bright elliptical ring around the central circle so that the whole thing looked like an eye or the planet Saturn surrounded by bright rings.

"That is what we've seen in our radio telescope-generated photos of various black holes across our galaxy and beyond. However, I think this particular singularity is too young to have gathered enough matter to form such a disc. It takes time. That an accretion disc will form is indisputable. Nature does not allow a naked singularity. Beyond the visible accretion disc and beyond the event horizon lies the singularity, forever hidden from human eyes." Ryan secretly congratulated himself for an explanation full of drama and mystery.

"But why is this hole here? Why here? Why now?" Fraser was intrigued.

"I have a hunch about that too, but I may be completely wrong."

"Go on. You're doing quite well so far," Anara encouraged him.

"Black holes are theorised to form in one of three ways. When a massive red giant star dies, that is its energy runs out. It is the fusion reaction inside it that keeps the matter expanded. So, once fusion stops, the matter starts coming together and the star collapses under its own gravity. However, there are no stars missing near our solar system so I think we can rule out this possibility. Such a star collapse also happens after a massive explosion like a supernova, wherein the outer layers are expelled, and again whatever remains coalesces into a black hole. Then again, we would not be standing here if a supernova explosion had happened here. It would have destroyed everything for light years around us, so that can also be discounted. Are you with me so far?" He was pleased to see everyone nod. He couldn't have made it any simpler. "The third cause can be when two stars in a binary system spiral in towards each other and collide forming what is called a torus. A torus is a closed, round surface with a black hole at its centre. With the same reasoning as earlier, we do not have any missing binary stars near us so we can rule this out as well.

"Which brings us to the last possibility." His eyes gleamed. He knew his hunch was right. Just the act of explaining the possibilities to his crew had given him both clarity and confidence. Anara had been right.

Explaining something did help to sort it out in one's own mind. "This involves high-energy collisions. A small black hole may be formed if particles of matter are accelerated to the speed of light and achieve sufficient density. It would have to be a massive amount of focused energy and an equally mammoth explosion."

"How would that happen here in outer space, Commander?" asked Manisha.

"Like I said, it would require a massive explosion, hundreds of times the energy we use in particle accelerators back on Earth to study the composition of matter. An explosion of sufficient magnitude equal to that between matter and antimatter."

"There is no way such a massive controlled explosion can take place in interstellar space. And wouldn't we have seen such an explosion?" Manisha persisted, not entirely convinced.

"You wouldn't see the explosion if it resulted in a black hole, because all the energy would be absorbed right back into it. And it would not need to be a controlled explosion."

"I'm not sure what you're leading us towards."

"I told you I had a hunch? Here is what I believe happened." He knew he was right even if he could not prove it. "I believe what we have here are the remnants of the TrueKif ship. Somehow—don't ask me how, I'm just speculating—the device Jim was carrying was set-off. Whether by accident or on purpose, we will never know. It could have compromised their matter-antimatter storage. A combined nuclear-plus-antimatter explosion happening at the speed of light? I can't even imagine the result. No one has ever thought of such a thing before. But it might just have compressed the ship and everyone in it into just the right size to form a singularity. Then," he sighed, "then it would have started absorbing matter and energy from space around it and continued to grow till it captured us as well."

There was a long silence as his audience digested this. Finally, Manisha said softly, "That's a horrible way to die. Compressed into nothingness."

Ryan smiled sardonically. "You may be right, but they may not even have known their deaths. It would have been instantaneous." He turned to Anara. "Captain, scientists far better than I will need years to unravel this particular mystery. It may even change FTL travel forever. If this is correct, then if any ship travelling at, or faster than the speed of light, explodes due to any reason, there is a real risk of formation of black holes. Spaceship designers will need to take extraordinary measures to prevent this, or humankind will have to learn to be satisfied with sub-light velocities. We will never reach the stars again!"

Fraser digested the information. "Let's just wait on that for a moment. You said the black hole sucks in all surrounding matter and energy. Does that mean it will continue to grow bigger and become more powerful?"

Anara was convinced that Ryan was right. They'd talked about all the possibilities. Now she had to deliver the bad news. "Most certainly it will, Colonel. It will continue to grow larger. Eventually it will be big enough to consume our sun and solar system, and then possibly we will have a nice accretion disc as well. It's just a matter of time."

11

Darkness Falls

"You're saying that it's not just we who are in danger. It is humanity itself and even the KifrWyss because this thing will keep expanding throughout this region of space across many light years, right?" Fraser looked stunned.

Anara nodded grimly. *I can't even save a hundred! How the hell did I just become responsible for saving eight billion lives?*

"How much time do we have? How much time does Earth have?" asked Manisha.

"Impossible to tell. We may have a few hours. Earth? A few months, a year. Possibly more. I have no way to tell," replied Ryan, as gently as he could.

"A *year*? That's *all*? Eight billion lives will be snuffed out within a year?"

Ryan nodded. "The people on Earth may not even know of the danger till it's too late. It will only become apparent when the effects of gravity start screwing up the solar system. Most likely, Earth will be destroyed long before it is absorbed, in a spectacular, if deadly, collision when the planets, moons and asteroids begin to get pulled out of their orbits."

Fraser had a vision of Mars and Earth colliding and annihilating each other. "Are you saying that there is no escape, Commander?"

"For us, or for Earth, Colonel?"

"Both, of course!"

"I don't see a way out. The gravity field generated is really intense, and all theories I have come across say that it is impossible to escape once you have entered the event horizon. Like I said earlier, our knowledge is limited, and our instruments are useless. We just don't know enough. We are the first humans to make contact with a black hole. Till date we have only observed miniature black holes in particle accelerators and they exist only for an infinitesimal short interval. Black holes have only been 'seen' indirectly through their effect on nearby systems, their gravitational waves or from simulated images from distant galaxies. We don't have direct measurements even from the supermassive black hole which we believe is at the centre of our own galaxy."

Anara paced the length of the room, observing the dismayed looks on the faces of her crew. She knew she did not have any hope to offer them. She had to keep trying even in the face of hopelessness. "Any way to determine the exact nature of this hole, Ryan? Will that help us?" she asked.

"I don't see how. Once matter or energy falls into the singularity it loses all identify and information. Everything reduces to the most basic of particles—all we can measure is the mass and possibly the momentum of the black hole. Every particle becomes the same. In essence, we will also be absorbed into one common pool. We will become part of the same universe," he answered, wishing he had something better to offer. "We need sufficient power to overcome the force of gravity pulling us in. The strongest we can generate is through our M-AM drive. And as we have seen, we were not able to achieve FTL velocity even with our M-AM drive."

Force? Explosion? Something clicked in Fraser's mind. "What about atom bombs, Commander? Will enough of them break the gravity hold? They pack a punch and we do have enough of them on board."

Ryan dearly wished he could offer more, but he was the ship's commander and a theoretical physicist, not a magician. There was nothing in the universe more powerful than a black hole. If anything, the energy from the bombs would be food for the giant. It could eat a hundred nuclear bombs for breakfast and still remain hungry. Anara and Ryan exchanged a look of understanding and disappointment. They were the leaders. They were supposed to give hope not take it away, even in the face of certain defeat.

"We do carry nukes, Colonel and we will certainly give them a try," agreed Anara.

Ryan shrugged his consent. The low lighting in the room and the eerie glow from the workstation screens made the perfect setting for the dark future they were heading into. Anara was right, he thought, there was no harm in trying the nukes, even though such devices only worked in science fiction movies. In fact, knowing the explosions would only fuel the craving of the black hole, he wasn't entirely sure that was a wise thing to do. He was glad the lack of lighting hid the dejected look on his face.

"Let's do it then. Manisha, line us up for firing. Let's start with two missiles. Dial them up for full ten megatons. Set for detonation at a thousand kilometres. Will that be enough?" Anara asked Ryan.

"Yep, that ought to do it. In normal space the explosion would not be dissipated by the lack of a medium. But inside the event horizon, the shock waves should travel away from us. Do we have enough power to put that distance between the bomb and us?

Last time we tried to move, we managed all of three hundred kilometres, remember?"

"We'll launch it towards the black hole and let gravity do the rest. It should move away faster than us."

"All right then. Manisha, let's get all engines up and running. Try to put as much distance between us and the bomb as you can."

"Yes, commander. Weapon will be ready in five minutes." She acknowledged his command but she realised, like Ryan, that the effort to move away would be futile. It had not worked the last time either. "Mr. Madhavan, you ready? We'll launch on my mark."

"Ready down here," replied Madhavan as his hands moved over the control station. He was pleased to see the engine status back in green. The ship was as ready as it would ever be especially after their last aborted attempt. "Don't let me down now," he whispered, caressing the controls.

"All ready for launch," reported Manisha, a few minutes later, studying her screen.

"Put up the display on the main holo." The centre of the room filled up with a simulated image of the ship in space with an estimate of the position of the centre of the black hole.

"Fire when ready," ordered Anara. This was it. In those three words she had ordered a nuclear launch.

In any other circumstances, she would have been responsible for genocide, but not today. Today she was trying to save billions of lives. She felt powerful and weak at the same time.

"Mark. Bomb away," called out Manisha.

"All engines engaged," reported Madhavan as the vibrations built up again and the ship once again struggled against the power of the hole.

The holo display showed the trajectory of the missile, and rapidly changing numbers scrolled along one side showing various data points.

"The missile is being pulled in and is accelerating," reported Ryan, his voice on edge. "I have lost lock. It was moving much faster than I anticipated. We may lose the ability to track it or even send the detonation signal. Recommend we send the signal now. The ship has barely moved but the missile should be at least five hundred kilometres away. It should be safe."

"The signal will also be moving inwards at the speed of light, but why take a chance? Do it!" Anara commanded.

Ryan pressed a button and they waited.

"Is it done?" asked Anara.

"Yes. Signal sent." Pressing a button to detonate a nuclear warhead seemed pretty anti-climactic to him.

Some members of the crew crowded the portholes.

Ryan was amused. They'd see nothing out of the window, but some might get hurt. "Everyone back to your stations. Strap in. We may get hit by a massive shock wave. Things will get rough." *Unlikely, but why take a chance?*

The crew obeyed and went back to their seats. Discipline won over curiosity.

"Well, where is my explosion?" demanded Anara after a few more seconds.

Manisha looked perplexed. "I don't understand. The missile should have exploded in microseconds on receiving the signal."

More seconds ticked by. Anara raised an eyebrow at Ryan. He shook his head.

A mild tremor rocked the massive ship.

"Is that it? I barely felt it?" remarked the Colonel.

Anara gave him a small nod. "The bulk of the force must've been directed towards the centre of the hole. It has probably been absorbed already. There isn't going to be anything more. We're lucky we felt as much as we did."

Fraser understood, but his mind refused to accept. "Will we get to know if it worked?"

"Let's wait and see if the gravitational pull reduces. That's the only way we can be sure. If the atomic explosion disrupts the singularity, there should be another explosion as the singularity releases all its stored mass and energy and then we would no longer be slaves to its gravity."

They waited. There was still hope, wasn't there? The holo however remained resolutely black. It had nothing to show.

"No explosions," sighed Ryan. "It didn't work."

"At least let's try pulling away one more time. Maybe your instruments are not working accurately." Fraser knew he was being stubborn, but he knew sometimes you needed to use brute force.

"Why? It's pointless. The singularity is right there." Ryan was irritated at the Colonel's doggedness.

Anara walked over to his side. "For the sake of the crew, Ryan. For the sake of the crew, let's test it."

"Okay," Ryan said with a nod. "Mr Madhavan. Fifty percent power. Reverse."

The engines were already primed. As Madhavan increased power, the ship struggled once more against gravity.

"It's not working, Captain. We are not moving. The explosion was a waste of two perfectly good atom bombs," reported Ryan.

"Well, we aren't exactly going to need them where we're going, are we?" Anara snapped. Then, she shook her head in frustration. "Alright. Alright. Power down. No point wasting fuel."

How many more disappointments will I have to suffer? I want to keep fighting but what's' the use? Is it time to roll up and surrender? Every theory I have read states it is impossible to escape the pull of a black hole. This is an impossible task. What's the point of fighting against the impossible? It would be so easy to just give up right now, right here.

***

Anara read through the details on her screen for the third time but found no new answers. She pushed back her chair and stared at the ceiling. Her room was considerably large by the ship's standards, yet she felt cramped. A desk, a couple of chairs, a small bureau, a concealed closet, a single bed along a wall. She was thankful for the open space in the centre of the room. The carpeted floor allowed her to continue her yoga routine on the days she could not hit the gym.

She looked up when Ryan knocked on the door and entered. He looked haggard and drawn.

"Tell me you have something else we can try?" asked Anara.

Ryan pulled up a chair and sat down. He shook his head in defeat. Anara had never seen him quite like this before. Ryan was her pillar, her cheerleader, her rock. Now, head bowed, he just sat there quietly.

The two of them reviewed in silence the virtual screen displaying the latest woefully inadequate data.

No signals were reaching the ship and while they were not completely blind, they were pretty close to it.

She pushed back her chair, walked to the porthole and looked outside. There was a beautiful show of lights outside. Streams of light appeared and disappeared seemingly at random. It was a fireworks' display in every colour of the rainbow. She'd expected a lot more red-shifting as the rays of light moved away from them and the frequency of light shifted lower and lower. But this was different. It was unexpected. They'd broken a barrier, entered a forbidden zone inside the event horizon. They were witnessing wonders never before revealed to the human eye. *But, rainbows? Inside the event horizon? What was happening? Well, at least our deaths will be pretty.*

A low murmur came from her virtual screen which flickered and blinked off. The subdued artificial lights dimmed as well, and Anara would later swear she saw the same light float out to space through the solid walls of the room, as if being sucked out by the black hole. She, however, convinced herself that it had been an illusion.

The room was now quite dark except for the irregular flashes from the exterior. Ryan had looked up in surprise at the sudden darkness, but he lowered his head again in resignation.

"Narada, what happened?" Anara called to the AI.

There was no reply. She felt the familiar vibrations of the ship's engines reduce considerably.

"Narada?" she called again. "Narada?" She almost punched the controls on her workstation in agitation.

"Ryan, snap out of it! I need your help. Narada seems to have gone offline!"

Ryan looked up slowly. "Yeah, must be the higher gravity finally starting to affect our power systems. We must be getting close to the singularity. It was expected."

To Anara's relief the emergency light came on suffusing the room in a soft red glow.

"What does this mean, Ryan? How close are we to the singularity? How much time do we have left?" It was then that she realised she had been avoiding facing the reality of their situation. She had, of course, been thinking about their predicament, about the black hole, but clinically, in an abstract manner. All the while, she had been evading the question—what would happen when they actually reached the singularity? How would they die? Now it hit her hard. This was happening. This was happening to her, the ship and the crew. They were at death's doorstep. There was no escape.

"I've already told you. I have no idea. Days, hours, minutes… take your pick."

"I'm not giving up yet. C'mon, let's go." She grabbed his shoulder, pulled him up and pushed him out of the room in front of her.

***

She had never seen Ops so quiet. No blinking lights, no active display screens, no hands actively working the controls. A few emergency lamps provided light but failed to dispel the gloom. Some members of the crew sat at their stations with nothing to do. They had no control. Everything was offline. *Antariksh* was adrift in space.

"Manisha, status report?"

"Primary controls not available. Backup controls have failed as well. Power at 32% of normal. Main computer is offline. AI is offline. Limited communication facilities available."

"What about the crew?"

"All accounted for as of ten minutes ago. A few bruises when the lights failed. Nothing major to report."

Anara watched out of the corner of her eyes as Ryan sat down at his station.

"Get me Madhavan," she commanded.

"Madhavan here," came the engineer's voice over the intercom.

"Status?"

"There was a sudden power drain on the engines, Captain. I've throttled down power to a bare minimum but if this continues we'll be out of fuel shortly. Most of the systems are offline."

"So the engines are still working? That's a relief."

"They are holding at 30% but I'm using up more fuel than normal. I'm not sure why. I'll keep checking and will get back to you."

"I'll take the small miracles for now. Okay, Manisha, I want everyone out of Ops and back in the quarters. Signal the crew to do the same. Then power down Environment to minimum. No point wasting more energy than we need to. Ryan, join me in the engine room with Madhavan, will you?

Ryan seemed to have regained some of his composure. He joined her as they followed the crew out of Ops.

"I'm sorry. My conduct was unbecoming earlier. I've let you down. You wanted solutions and there is nothing more I can offer you today."

"Listen to me, Ryan." She pulled him by his arm. "We are still in command. We do not, *cannot,* give up. A hundred people depend on us to keep trying. They will all die the second we give up. There are another eight billion innocent people back on Earth who also depend on us. I noticed how the crew was looking at you back in Ops. They were frightened. They thought you were giving up. That's not fair to them. They derive courage from us. They derive strength from our actions and our composure. They derive hope from us. You know what I have learnt in the last few days, sitting alone in my room? We live on hope. We thrive on hope. Hope makes us chase our dreams and hope is what defines us humans. You cannot take away their hope." She cupped his face in her palms and looked into his eyes. "I will not let this crew down and neither will you, got it? Even if there is absolutely nothing more to be done, even then," she paused to compose herself, "even then we... we will die with dignity giving it everything we've got and then a little more."

She let him go and started walking. Ryan followed her, his steps a little firmer, his back a little straighter.

They reached engineering.

"Are you ready? Are you with me, Ryan?" She knew what his answer would be, but she needed to her it from him.

He nodded. "Let's do this."

***

"Madhavan, your report?" Anara ordered as soon as she entered Engineering and located him.

"All non-essential systems have been shut down," he replied, pausing his frantic activities. "I've kept environment controls working. Heat and light are just about what the engines can manage. I might be able to get more power for a short duration, but the fuel consumption will not be worth the effort. Higher power outputs just seem to drain our energy faster. The devil outside is devouring us. Right now, my priority is conserving fuel. I know you will try to break us free again. I know you. And I'm making sure the ship is ready for you. You are going to try, aren't you?"

Anara spoke to him in a soft voice. "We've tried everything, Madhavan. Ryan and I are out of ideas. I was hoping you'd have something."

"All I can give you is a bit of power for a few more hours. I'm sorry. I can fix any engine, propel any ship. I know the intricacies of faster-than-light travel. I deal in gravity generators, but I don't know how to escape this… this singularity. It is stronger than anything I have ever faced before. I guess what I'm saying is, tell me your plan and I'll find a way to make it happen."

"That's that then, Ryan," Anara looked at Ryan. "Nothing else left to try." She shook her head wearily then smiled wanly. "We will die with dignity, right?" She smiled wanly. "We should tell the crew to get mentally ready. This ship may be our tomb but let's give them a chance to get prepared."

12

The Last Hour

Her crew received the news of their pending destruction with surprising equanimity. Everyone had been granted leave to spend the time they had left in whichever way they saw fit. How does one prepare for death?

***

Colonel Fraser decided to take a last walk amidst his weaponry. He touched the shiny side of the fast attack flyer, feeling the smooth cold metal with his fingers. The dark, aerodynamic shape of the flyer always gave him a sense of power. The multiple machine guns, rocket launchers, guided munitions, laser guns. The flyer could impose justice. But not this time. He thought about the troops he was supposed to be leading. They were never going to fight the battles they'd trained so hard for. This time they were up against an enemy they could not fight, an enemy they did not even understand.

***

Dr Khan put away his instruments one last time. The medical room was prepared to receive casualties but somehow, he didn't believe there would be any. He thought about Lucy and her baby. He smiled when he remembered holding the baby in his arms. Baby Anara, named after her mother's saviour. He hoped the two of them and Joe would remain safe on Earth. He would pray for their long life.

***

Madhavan walked around Engineering. He felt contented here, among the soothing vibrations of his engines. He had promised the Captain he would keep them running if she needed the power. He still believed she would find a way. Till then he would tend to the engines and keep the crew warm and comfortable.

***

Ryan thought about his wife, Joan, and his daughter, Sophia. They would be waiting for him to come back home and they would keep waiting forever. No. Not forever. Only till the black hole consumed the entire solar system. He had hardly spent any time at home over the last two years. On the last visit home, he'd met them briefly before being called to Mumbai to stop the two aliens. His daughter was growing up so fast. This was not fair. If he could only find a way to destroy this monstrosity, he could at least save his family back on Earth.

***

Manisha held Kevin's hand, stroking it gently, lost in her thoughts. It had seemed so natural to her to seek him out and find solace in his company. Accelerated romance, she thought, but it felt comfortable. It felt like just the right thing to do. She folded her legs beneath herself and rested her head on Kevin's shoulders. Was this love or just the need for emotional support? She did not know and did not care. They would all be dead in a few hours and life would go on everywhere else. Till the black hole reached everywhere else.

Kevin sat motionless. This had never happened to him before. He felt content and fulfilled. His free hand stroked Manisha's hair, while he wondered what his next step would be. Oh, chuck it, he thought, then bent forward, pulled up her face slowly and kissed her. It was love's first kiss, not a lovers' kiss. Filled with passion yet restrained, unsure. She kissed him back and he relaxed. It was going to be all right.

Manisha's eyes widened, then she closed them, savouring the surprise. It felt so natural. She let go of her fears, lost in the moment. But something still nagged at her—why did the Captain give up the fight? Anara never threw in the towel, whatever be the odds stacked against her. Why now? Why this time? Captain Anara needed a push, Manisha decided. *I've just found Kevin. I'm too bloody young to die!*

***

A single candle burned in Anara's room as she sat cross-legged on the carpeted floor. She had left her hair loose and it cascaded over her shoulders. Her eyes were closed as she worked to control her breathing and relax her mind. As usual, she was unsuccessful. Outwardly, she was calm but her mind raced in all directions and random thoughts kept breaking her concentration.

She thought of her early childhood; she had been protected, yet had always felt driven to try new experiences. She recalled the names of her friends from school. She remembered her training in the Air Force and the day she'd been selected for space training at ISC after one failed attempt. The thrill of her first space flight. The sorrow over the loss of the entire crew of *Akash-2* when it had crashed on Mars. And of course, the last two eventful years.

She felt like a person being led to the gallows: the knowledge her time would soon be up and the utter helplessness to do anything about it. *Death is the only constant.*

There was a soft knock on her door. It was repeated when she did not respond.

"Come in," she called out. The door slid open and Manisha hesitatingly poked her head inside.

"Do you have a minute?"

"Sure. Come in. Feeling alone? Would you like some tea? I made a pot."

"No, thank you. I had something on my mind, thought I'd come over and see if you were up for a short talk."

"You mean you have something on your mind besides Kevin?" Anara smiled softly. The young woman's secret was not a secret aboard the ship. Come join me," said Anara patting the floor in front of her. ""Do you know how to sit in the *padmasana,* lotus pose? Here I'll show you." She helped Manisha cross her legs and position her hands in the proper posture.

The flame of the candle fluttered creating moving shadows in the room before settling down again to a steady glow. Manisha stared at the flame as if she had never seen fire before.

Anara observed her through half open eyes. *She has come as a troubled young woman, not a military officer.*

"I hate this waiting," Manisha said, with a sigh. "Why are we still floating around? We entered the event horizon hours ago. We should have reached the singularity by now at the speed of light."

"What do you mean?"

"We move at the speed of light once we enter the event horizon, don't we? Under the gravity hold of the singularity?"

"No, no. That's not correct. Our speed increases as we accelerate but we don't reach the speed of light, at least not till we reach the end, I believe."

"Oh. I thought..." Manisha's voice trailed off.

They sat staring at the flame.

"What do you think awaits us?"

"I do not know, Manisha," replied Anara trying not to alarm the young woman any further. "This is another first for humankind, being absorbed by a black hole. But I guess there is no better way to become one with the universe, don't you think?"

"If you say so, but..." her voice trailed off. "But, you know, I never expected you to give up, Captain. You have always fought against the greatest odds. Why not now? Why are you accepting this... this... fate?"

"There are times, Manisha, when a person should recognize the futility of her struggles. Maybe this is my time. God knows we have tried every option we could think of."

"I can't believe those are your words."

"Ahh," Anara answered, her voice gentle. "It is the burden of leadership, Manisha. Sometimes even fearless spaceship captains must give up when the odds are stacked up impossibly against them. But all of us, we are together in this. We are calm and collected and we will face whatever comes together. Sometimes we should accept our destiny with courage and pray for strength to face whatever fate has in store for us."

Manisha lowered her eyes. Some of her assertiveness left her. She stood up slowly.

Anara felt a twinge of guilt for having broken the young officer's trust. She felt sorry for having let down her entire crew, a hundred souls who had trusted her to bring them home safe.

Manisha stood up. At the door, she turned around.

"You know I had read somewhere that black holes are actually not just singularities, but portals or doorways."

"Uh-huh?"

"They might be wormholes which can transport us many light years away or even into a parallel universe or maybe even another dimension. Maybe we won't die. Have you thought of this?"

Anara stood up, went to Manisha and put her hands on her shoulders, looking deep into her black eyes. She wished she were young again. *Oh, for the energy and optimism, the defiance, of youth!*

"Manisha, I understand your need to believe so, but none of those theories have been definitively proven."

"Maybe the theories haven't been proven but they have not been disproven either. For that matter who has proved the singularity theory beyond all doubt? What makes that theory valid and not my belief?"

"You were in Ops with me when we tried to escape. You have seen all the data, all the observations."

"Observations and data are not everything. What about faith? What about curiosity and open-mindedness. I mean, look at it this way, if a black hole absorbs all matter and radiation, then where does it all go? How can all of it be compressed into a space of zero volume?"

"All matter is mostly empty space; as much as 99.9%. Even the basic building blocks may finally be made up only of pure energy. Maybe the old string theory was correct after all. Maybe everything gets converted to some form of exotic energy. And energy does not require volume. Or maybe the singularity just squeezes all matter till there is no more empty space between the basic particles—"

"No. I don't think what you're saying is right. Even if matter is compressed there *has* to be a limit to the compression. I can't subscribe to the accepted theory even if you do. I believe the black hole is a portal and if it is, then we can pass through it unscathed."

Anara dropped her hands from Manisha's shoulders. She had nothing that could counter the burning conviction in Manisha's eyes.

"Maybe that is so," she said, trying to end the debate, "but we have no way to prove it. Even if I agree that this black hole is really a portal, we still cannot pass through it. The gravity will stretch, and tear us apart even before we can reach its centre."

"You're just gonna roll over and die? Accept your fate and refuse to do anything more? I'm sorry, but I expected more from you. I trusted that you, of all people, would hold out and resist. The Captain I knew would have pushed back even against gravity if she could." Her voice dripped with disappointment.

Anara froze, staring at her. "What did you say?"

Manisha hesitated. She knew she'd gone too far.

"I'm sorry. I didn't mean to get emotional."

"No, no. Not that." Anara took her by the shoulders and shook her hard. "What were the exact words you used? 'Push back against gravity'?"

Manisha nodded.

"Anti-gravitons! You're a genius, Manisha. Come with me." Anara rushed out of the room, Manisha in tow. "And better start praying you're right about that portal!"

13

A New Hope

They ran down the deserted, darkened corridors, Manisha close behind Anara.

"Where are we going?" Manisha panted.

"To test your scheme. You'd better be right. I don't think we have much time left."

Anara came to a sudden stop in front of a door and Manisha bumped hard into her.

"S... Sorry," she said, rubbing her right forearm.

Anara paid no heed to her apology and banged hard on the door.

"Ryan! Ryan! Open up. We've got work to do!"

The door opened to reveal a somewhat dishevelled-looking Commander.

"Captain? What's the ...?"

Before he could conclude, Anara had grabbed him with both hands and had already started pulling him down the corridor.

"I'll explain everything along the way. C'mon!"

"At least let me get my shoes!"

"We don't have the time. Manisha, go to Ops and get the senior staff assembled. Wait for my orders. Tell Colonel Fraser to come down to Engineering and meet me. Got it? Go!"

"Yes, ma'am," said Manisha and peeled off down another corridor. Captain Anara was back, and it felt good to have a purpose even if it was just following orders.

Anara and Ryan hurried towards Engineering in the light of the emergency lamps.

"Just what is going on with you, Captain?"

"You explained all those details about black hole. You also mentioned a charged or Kerr black hole through which we might be able to travel. What was that all about?" She paused to catch her breath. "This black hole might contain a singularity and all of us have taken this fact for granted, but what if we consider an alternate theory, that it is a doorway to a wormhole or... or a fracture in spacetime? If we can find a way to travel through it, we might yet pull through."

"Stop!" Ryan pulled her up short at the entrance to the engine room. "Let me get this straight. You want to try and go *through* a black hole?" he asked, incredulous. "Yes, it is theoretically possible to travel through a Kerr type of black hole. Yes, it may contain a wormhole or portal as you say. But what you are proposing just can't be done, Kerr-type black hole or not. Our very act of entering the black hole will disturb it irrevocably. You can't seriously be thinking of making it through unscathed?"

"Ryan! Listen to me. We are going to die anyway and as a young woman just reminded me, she depends on me to provide a solution. A way out. We have to push back. So what if the theory seems absurd? No human has ever encountered a black hole before us, so who really knows what transpires inside one of them? For all we know there could be the devil waiting for us inside or God even. There is zero empirical evidence to support any of the theories, including that of the devil for that matter, so how do you conclude which one is correct?"

"We can't," he agreed somewhat reluctantly.

"Great! Now that that is settled let's stop wasting time and get the evidence we need—by living the moment. You said that our effort might disturb the hole. I think a portal, if it is present, may be minuscule. We need to find a way to open the aperture wider.

Make it bigger and keep it open till *Antariksh* can pass through it."

"You want *Antariksh* to thrust against the gravity of the black hole... to...to create a corridor. A tunnel?"

"Exactly!" This was why she admired Ryan. He was smart. He just needed to be given a nudge in the right direction sometimes.

"It's like those stents they used to put in the human body to keep blocked blood vessels open. If we can generate a strong enough field, we might be able to create enough space for us to get through. *Antariksh* will be out stent. It will be our wedge and our vessel. We can create an inverse gravity field, right? You did say this was a young black hole. It might just be weak enough for our plan to work. And the gravity field will keep us suspended inside the portal or wormhole similar to the repulsion between similar poles of a magnet. If we do not interact with the wormhole, we will not disturb it. It can work!"

Ryan looked at her, shook his head as if still trying to digest all she had said and then nodded. *Oh, what the hell! Once more unto the breach. Better to do something than to sit in the cabin moping away.*

Anara pushed the button to open the doors.

The first sight to greet them was that of her engineer Madhavan slumped over his station his head buried in his hands.

My God. What have I done? I have let the life go out of my team.

"Madhavan! Get up. I've got the idea you wanted so badly."

The engineer looked up and right past them, as if unable to focus. She walked across and shook him hard. "Gather yourself, mister. You can grieve all you want later."

"Yes. Yes. You are back. You have a plan? I was waiting for you to come back. I am ready. The engines are ready. What exactly are we doing again?"

The door opened again and Colonel Fraser walked in, followed by Kevin, both of them locking fresh in their crisp uniforms. Anara almost smiled. *The cavalry was also here.*

"You called, Captain?"

"Yes, sir. I need your help. We need to get all our people prepared and alert for a manoeuvre we are going to attempt. I can't spare anyone from my staff, and your people are best suited for the job. You have to get everyone on this ship into the *dome*. I'll give more instructions later once we have set up."

Fraser nodded, turned on his heels and left with Kevin.

Military personnel do take took orders well, provided they are delivered with authority.

"Now, Ryan, how do we do this?"

14

Through The Looking Glass

"Will one of you please fill me in too?" moaned Madhavan, who was nursing a huge tension headache. "Just what do you want from me?"

Ryan looked over at Anara. "All yours."

"Always," she responded with equal sarcasm.

"Okay, Mr. Madhavan. We need to reconfigure our gravity generators to invert our gravity field. It'll require several steps, am I right?"

"Invert? Why?"

"Well," Ryan said. "The Captain here believes that we can travel through the black hole, find a wormhole and travel to another universe."

"Sure. Sure, I can invert the field. And you can tell me why we are really doing this while we work? How much time do we have?" In his current state, he did not even try to make sense of what was being said.

Ryan wished he knew the answer. "No idea. Sensors are no longer working. I could look out of the window and tell you, if that'll help. Anyway, I need your undivided attention for just a few minutes while our control systems are still functioning. We owe it to the crew to give this our best shot, right?"

"Okay. I'll... I'll re-align the graviton particle emitters, you go ahead and set up the calibration. What power levels do you need?" Some of the requirements filtered through into his clouded mind. This was just the kind of problem that got Madhavan right back on track and raring to go.

"Let's see." Ryan tried pulling up a screen which flickered weakly. He grabbed a tablet and pen, to ensure he did not make a mistake in their calculations. Writing also helped him focus his thoughts. "At faster-than-light speeds, we generate a substantial gravity field bending the space around us. Maximum level of gravitons we can emit will be approximately 125%. We might be able to push that by a few more points so say 130%."

"Sure that'll be enough?" asked Anara.

"The gravity field outside we last measured was 85% of our maximum level. At the rate of increase we'd observed earlier, in the last thirty minutes it should have reached 110% or more by now. So, yeah, 130% should be enough. That's still thousands of times Earth's gravity. Hopefully, we will be at the singularity by that time. Best estimates only, of course."

"Go ahead. I'm off to see the preparations of the ship and crew. Do I have ten minutes from you?"

"This procedure will eat up our fuel pretty fast. I don't think I can hold this for more than that. Better hurry."

"If this doesn't work then we won't need the fuel for we will die here in this space. If it does work and we do get to our normal space we may still have enough fuel to limp home at the very least. It's a calculated risk. Now, you can turn off power to all the sections and I will get everyone into the *dome.*"

Ryan looked at her, wondering if that was the last time they would see each other, but he could not allow emotions to sway him from his task. "Roger, but I'm not sure we will be joining you. Someone needs to be here. Madhavan and I can manage this end. One more thing, don't activate the *dome.* It protects us from time dilation. We are already inside the event horizon. To outside observers, time is flowing more slowly for us than for them. The *dome* will mess up time flow for the people inside, I think. We are better off not using it. Besides, we just don't have any power to spare for its operation."

"You sure of this?"

"About as sure as I am about this whole hare-brained scheme. It is a good idea to keep the people together in the *dome,* but don't activate it. Just trust me on this, okay?"

The ship vibrated strongly.

"What was that?" asked Anara, holding on to a table for support.

"We must be getting closer. I feel heavier. And look at that panel. Our artificial gravity is no longer required. Our protection systems are being overwhelmed. We need to get gravity inverted now! Get the crew prepared, Captain. Go now! Madhavan, we need to move."

"Best of luck," she called out as she ran out of Engineering.

The two men worked feverishly, running from station to station to activate the gravity field.

"Ready at my end. You done?" called out Ryan, a few minutes later.

"Activating now!" answered Madhavan.

***

A skeleton crew led by Manisha was holding the fort in Ops. *At least I can say my goodbyes,* Manisha thought, glancing around. She hesitated, then pressed the intercom button. "Kevin," she whispered.

"Manisha? Are you okay? I so wanted to talk to you. Listen, you left the lounge so suddenly. I'm sorry about what happened in there. But I really like you. You hear? I really like you and…"

"Kevin, I know. I wish we had more time. But, if we do manage to survive this passage, then…" Her voice broke, and she closed her eyes tightly. "Stay safe. Goodbye." She closed the circuit.

***

The Colonel had managed to gather the rest of the crew in the *dome*. Anara joined them to find most people sitting around listlessly. Most were silent, though a few quiet sobs could be heard in the semi-darkness. They were sapped of energy, just wanting it to be over. *Time to play captain.*

"Listen people," she said, speaking in a loud, confident tone. "I know things have been chaotic, but through it all you have been an amazing crew. We believed... *I* believed we would escape. But we could not," Her voice shook a little, but she gathered her courage and continued. "As it stands; we believe we are very close to the singularity, the centre of the black hole. Perhaps this is the end, but there may yet be another way out. I'm asking for your support one more time." She looked at her crew with pride as they listened to her intently, most of them now standing up. "Now, we do not know what will happen in the next few minutes, so we prepare as if we are going to face an intense storm in space. I want you to stay in pairs to help each other. Buckle up or hold on tight to something. Preferably, something that is be fixed to the floor. Stow away or remove anything movable that could hurt somebody. Got it? Let's hustle! Colonel Fraser, you're with me. We will seal the room as soon as the crew is ready."

In less than a minute they were ready with most of the crew sitting in pairs on either side of the pods, holding on to the structure, waiting for the unknown.

***

The space outside churned with a maelstrom of colours. Light performed a strange dance of luminosity and darkness, intermixed with a swirling tempest of particles. The lack of windows prevented the crew from looking outside, and most of them missed a sight never before seen by human eyes. For a brief instant, even the *dome,* despite being deep inside the ship, lit up in beautiful colours, and then just as suddenly everything went black. This darkness was complete and not even a speck of light was visible. The brightness was complete too, devouring away the last traces of black and penetrating every particle of matter in the room. It seemed to permeate through the very skin of people such that they seemed to have an ethereal glow.

Very few could keep their eyes open in the face of such fearsome beauty. Nobody chose to except one.

Anara's natural curiosity overcame her fear and she tried to watch through hooded eyes.

I have to see this sight.

Everyone else cowered down, their eyes shut tight, but Anara opened her eyes wide for a second, taking it all in before being forced to close them tightly. *So, this is what a singularity feels like. Squeezed into a single point of no volume. Only a supremely courageous, a supremely foolish person or a supremely unlucky person like myself will ever see this again.* She was surprised to find that she was smiling. *If this is death, it is exquisite.*

The ship rocked ever so slightly as it crossed some invisible threshold. Then the vibrations grew progressively stronger. *Antariksh* started to rotate as the engines struggled to keep it steady. After a point, they failed altogether leaving the ship and its crew at the mercy of the savage behemoth that knew no emotions except hunger, the insatiable hunger to devour every particle of matter it managed to grasp.

The ship was now in freefall, gyrating with the turbulence outside. It spun faster and faster throwing everyone off their feet. Many of the crew lost their handholds and were flung about. They fell on each other and against the walls breaking more than a few bones. The room filled with groans and screams as the reality finally hit home, and hard. The end was here.

Then, it stopped. Their swirling motion just stopped. The darkness melted away as a blazing radiation suffused them all. Their bodies seemed to be turning translucent. Brighter and brighter, the light became till the crew, the ship, and everything inside turned transparent.

They had entered the black hole.

Their mass was being converted into the very basic building blocks of matter, smaller than atoms. Smaller than electrons or quarks or leptons. They were turning into pure energy. The black hole embraced them, soaking up their essence.

It was all over.

15

The Singularity

The calmness was deep.

The silence was complete.

Space was harmonious.

No stray particles disturbed the tranquillity. No photons of light traipsed about disturbing the serenity.

There was no fear here, but neither was there any hope, sadness, love, or cheer. Space was primeval.

Time did not flow.

There was no beginning and no end.

There was just the singularity.

All was one.

16

The Universe

She was part of the Entity. One with the vast Cosmos. The balance was captivating. She was one of most fundamental particles, and yet she was pure energy. The secrets of the atom were exposed to her, and yet she knew the scale of the cosmos as well.

Speed was irrelevant. Time was irrelevant. Life was irrelevant.

She was here, and she was everywhere. She was at the singularity and yet she could see herself entering the singularity. She saw the Big Bang and the birth of the universe. She saw its frozen death, when its energy had been exhausted and all was cold. Deathly cold. So cold that she would have frozen solid, had she a body.

She saw worlds being formed and other worlds ending. She saw the birth of stars and their death in black holes. She did not understand how she saw; after all she did not have any eyes or a body. She travelled through galaxies and found life everywhere. And she found death in equal measure. She reached the edge of the universe and could go no further. She sensed something beyond it. Tantalizingly out of reach. *Was there a boundary to the universe as well, or were there many universes spreading out... into what?*

She saw her own birth and she wanted to see how she would die and whether there was life after death. Something tugged at her heart. *But I have no heart?* Something called her back. *No,* she protested. *I want to see my death. The secret is out there. Let me go!*

The darkness was fading. The tranquillity, the peace was fading as well. Someone was groaning in pain. No, screaming in agony. Not just one person. There were many voices and she sensed fear and confusion and wanted to reach out. To help them. To support them. To tell them that everything would be all right.

The delicate balance vanished and she fell.

17

Affliction

The screams of the wounded in the background nearly deafened her. Someone seemed to be calling her, but she could barely make out the words. She wanted to go back to peace, but something was pulling her back to reality. *Let me go!*

"Captain! Captain Anara! Wake up! C'mon. Don't you dare die on me," Ryan shook her hard. Then another pair of hands appeared, helping Ryan. Madhavan.

They stood back as an automated nurse jolted her with electricity, trying to get her heart working again. "She is breathing. I have a pulse. Steady heartbeat. Please get her into a comfortable position while I call the doctor for a check-up." The voice was flat, mechanical, but it well suited the shiny bulbous body with multiple limbs. An automaton designed to support the doctor on board.

Ryan and Madhavan carried Anara to a corner, and lay her down carefully. Ryan made a pillow with his jacket under her head.

She opened her eyes slowly, still in the midst of her dream.

Had it been a dream or something else entirely? Wait, why can't I see anything?

In a moment of sheer panic, she jolted upright, flailing her arms wildly against whoever was holding her.

"Wha...what happened?" Her words came out in a croak.

"Thank god you're all right. I thought we'd lost you. You just refused to wake up. Doctor! over here!" Ryan called out.

"Ryan, it's you, but why is everything so dark?" She struggled to rise but her body failed to support her efforts.

Ryan pushed back her hair from her face, trying to soothe her. There was chaos all around. The room was full of people, the wounded lying on the floor or on makeshift stretchers, some leaning against the walls. Medical teams assisted by volunteers moved swiftly among them. The severely wounded had already been moved out to the medical bay, but that facility had quickly been overwhelmed. The other patients would have to be kept in the *dome* till other arrangements could be made. The worst aspect was the screaming.

Dr Khan finished with the crewman he'd been attending to, and hurried over.

He quickly checked Anara and was pleased not to find any major injuries, though there were any number of cuts and bruises all over her body. He shone a light in her eyes but she did not react.

"Can you hear me, Captain?"

"Of course I can. But I can't see anything. Where am I?"

"You're still in the *dome*. We've converted this into a medical triage facility. A number of crew persons have been hurt during our descent through the black hole." Dr Khan was concerned about the eyes, but at least she seemed okay otherwise.

"The black hole!" Realization dawned on her. *Yes, we were entering a black hole and then there were lights and there was peace. Peace, after a long, long time.* "We've escaped? We're alive?"

"You betcha we're alive," Ryan smiled. "It worked. Your strategy worked. You saved the ship and the crew."

"Then why is everyone screaming? Why are they in pain?"

"All in good time." Dr Khan said. "Right now, I'm going to ask you to close your eyes and rest right here. There are other people who are facing a similar issue with their sight. It might be an effect of our travel, but I need to carry out more tests to be sure. Right now, you will rest. I'll be back, Commander. Give her fluids to drink, will you?" Dr Khan disappeared as quickly as he had come.

"What happened, Ryan?" asked Anara as she struggled to sit up. Ryan handed her a sphere. The membrane of the sphere melted in her mouth releasing the cool, refreshing, fortified water inside. She gulped down the water and asked for more. It felt good, the sphere popping in her mouth. Ryan supported her back as she sighed with relief and leaned against his arm. He helped prop her up against a wall.

"It seems the black hole was a Kerr type charged black hole, after all. We went through it and emerged on the other side." Ryan grinned. "I never would have believed it, but it worked."

"You can thank Manisha for the idea. Where are we? And how is the crew?" She turned her head around trying to make sense of the din surrounding her. "They need me. I must go check on them. What did Dr Khan mean when he said they've lost their sight?"

"Relax," said Ryan, pushing her back gently. "Everyone is accounted for and being looked after by the medical teams. You are the last one to wake up, it seems. The crew is safe for now. A few cracked skulls and quite a few broken bones, but there have not been any critical injuries. Some of the crew seem to have been blinded. The doctor believes it is temporary possibly due to the intense lights we encountered inside the wormhole. He doesn't know the specific reason yet."

"What happened to us, Ryan? Where are we right now?"

"It's very confusing. We're still trying to figure it out, but right now, I must get back to Engineering. The engines are dead, and we're completely drained of all antimatter for the fuel. We are running on backup power only. I have to try and get some generators going or we are looking at a very cold death in this place, wherever this is. Don't worry, I'll send Manisha to sit with you. She can brief you while I see to the generators, okay?"

She nodded. Her head had started pounding and she felt disoriented. The darkness did not help one bit. She was grateful for a few moments of rest. She closed her eyes. *Blindness. That's all I needed right now. How the hell am I going to command the ship? Should I handover control to Ryan? Maybe this is temporary. I am not injured otherwise. Let's wait and see how this develops. I hope the crew will remain safe.*

***

She must have fallen asleep for some time. The place was quieter. She could sense much less movement of people. *Damn, I still can't see anything!* She rubbed her eyes hard till another pair of hands stopped her. They felt soft, feminine.

"Is that you, Manisha?"

"Yes, ma'am. I'm right here." Manisha had made sure Kevin was alright, even giving him a quick hug, on her way over from Ops to help the Captain. She could hardly believe they were all alive.

"Were you hurt?" Anara asked.

"No. I'd strapped myself in just as we went through. I was more fortunate than most other people. You want some more water?"

"Not right now, thank you. You were in Ops during the transit, weren't you? Tell me our status. Where exactly are we and how is the ship?"

"I don't have all the data yet; most of the instruments are down. But it seems my hunch was correct. The black hole was literally a hole, a portal if you wish. We managed to push through it and, like Alice, we are in a different world."

"Different world? You're not making sense."

"This world, this place is not making sense, Captain. I'm afraid that's the best description I can give you. You see, there is nothing out there outside this ship. No stars, no energy reading, no particles—nothing. I don't know if we are still inside the singularity and if so, how we are alive and kicking. Or have we fallen into a parallel universe or even another dimension? Roll the dice and take your pick, as the Commander would say. However, we...we did manage to survive and that, for me, is enough for the moment."

"And *Antariksh*?"

"Undamaged as far as we can tell, though we have no engines and no power as Commander Ryan must've informed you already. Fortunately, we do have enough power backup for the next couple of days at least."

"What else?" Anara closed her eyes. She realised that it made no difference whether they were open or closed. This blindness would take some time to get used to. She hoped it was only temporary.

"I just don't know. I have been trying to get some more sensors working and then maybe we'll get some answers. For now, we are dead in the proverbial water."

***

An hour later, sufficiently recovered but still thankful for the support of Manisha's shoulder, Anara stepped back into Ops. Manisha eased her into her chair and went back to work at her station.

"Talk to me, Manisha. Anything further on the sensors?"

Manisha worked her controls. "I have basic sensors working Captain, but I have limited the range to conserve power. I had set the system to scan the space around us for five million kilometres. Like I'd told you earlier, there is nothing out there."

"You keep saying 'nothing'. What do you mean *nothing*? How far are we from the solar system?"

"No. You don't understand. There is literally *nothing* out there. I mean there are no stars, no planets, and no celestial bodies of any kind. My instruments don't even show any energy readings. There is nothing out there except complete darkness."

"That is not possible. Even the deepest reaches of space have something—distant stars, a few atoms, photons of light. Check again."

"I am telling you, ma'am. I've checked everything three times. There is nothing here. Look for yourself. Nothing." She winced, realizing her mistake. The Captain could not see. "I'm sorry."

"It's okay," Anara waved away the apology. "What about the vision systems? The radio telescopes? What do they show?"

"Nothing. The images are blank. No radiation, no stars in deep space."

It had to be something wrong with the instruments.

"Call Madhavan. Tell him to take the sensors apart if he has to. Find out where we are and how do we get back to Earth from here. Ask Ryan to meet me here once he's free. Meanwhile, read through to me all the parameters you have tested so far."

***

"How're you feeling?" Ryan asked. Anara looked pale. It would have been better if she'd rested for some time. Instead, here she was poring over scraps of data that Manisha read out loud. It was so much more difficult to make sense of figures and equations when she could not see them flowing before her eyes. Yet, she had persisted.

"I'm fine," she said shrugging off his concern. "Find anything new?"

"We might be able to get the engines working in a few hours but, with hardly any fuel reserves, we're stuck." He leaned in closer to her. "There is something seriously wrong. I don't think we have come out of the black hole into normal space. We are trapped, I don't know where."

"Yeah, Manisha told me as much. Do you have a plan?"

"I was hoping that we could work out our options once you were strong enough."

"I'm strong enough to work. Blindness does not make me useless. Besides the doctor did say it was temporary, right? Okay, for the moment this is what I propose we do. We avoid causing panic at all costs. The crew must be disturbed and, with so many injured, we must be shorthanded. We can't let them know just yet that the leadership is as lost as the ship. Let's keep this strictly on a need-to-know basis. Restrict access to Ops to the senior officers only. We may need to set up a secondary station for the non-essential personnel. Once Madhavan has checked out the sensors get him to relay all the data to Ops. We will work out of here. Get to work, will you, Ryan? I want to go check on the crew. I'll be back shortly. You too, Manisha, not a word to anyone. Now help me to Medical."

***

Anara walked into Medical, her hand on Manisha's shoulder for guidance.

"Hey, Doc. I need an update."

"You really shouldn't be walking around. Let me get you into examination."

"Don't worry about me, Doc. I'm holding up. Tell me, how's the crew?"

"They're doing well for the most part. Fourteen broken legs and arms being set. They'll be fine by morning and will be able to resume duties shortly. Eight crewmembers with fractured skulls but no internal injury. The regeneration will be complete in a few hours. Four people with concussions, recovered and sent back to work. We've patched up quite a few cuts and bruises but we seem to have been fortunate. Except…"

"Except the blindness? Did you find the cause or a cure? How many are affected?"

The doctor did not answer. He looked down, arranging various instruments on the tray. "That's got me slumped. Can you step over here for a minute? Let me check you out."

Anara settled into a chair while Dr Khan, ran a few tests on her eyes. In hindsight, it had been irresponsible to open her eyes to witness the transit through singularity. But that act had allowed her to experience something profound. She could not share that with anyone, though. Not right now.

"There is nothing physiologically wrong with your eyes. Can you see nothing? Not even this?" He flashed a powerful flashlight directly into her eyes.

"No. It's completely dark."

He switched off the light. *At least her mind remains strong. That is what really matters.* "You are remarkably composed about the whole incident, aren't you?"

Anara gave a small laugh. "I might still be in shock or maybe I have seen too much destruction, no? Anyway, do you have any ideas?"

"Like I said, there is nothing wrong with your eyes, just like with the other six people. The intense light may have overcome the retina during the crossing, or maybe there is some electrical disruption in your nerves which is not allowing the signals to travel to your brain. I will need to study this more."

"You think this is temporary?"

"I cannot say for sure, but I believe so. Flash blindness is a well-known visual impairment. It is caused when intense light over-saturates the retina. It generally fades over time and I'm hoping that is the case. Some of the crew affected earlier seem to be recovering. Maybe you just need more time. I'm sorry I can't help you more. I'll start the tests. If I can learn more from your results, maybe I can work out a course of treatment, okay?"

"No. No tests on me. I've got too much to do. Get one of the other crew members."

The ear-piercing scream from the bed behind them made them jump. A second later a second person screamed.

The doctor ran over. "Nurse, sedative, fifteen milligrams, quickly!" It took them some time to get the two patients under control and settled down.

"What was that?"

"PTSD—Post Traumatic Stress Disorder, most likely. Quite a few of the crew are dealing with mental trauma right now, as am I quite frankly. It's not every day that one passes through a black hole. I've given them some sedative. They'll sleep for some time."

"Yeah, about that? Will you be able to find what really happened during our wormhole transit and if there are any residual effects on the human body?"

"I'll get to it, but I have a feeling it can be explained more by physics than by medicine."

18

Zero Space

"I've checked all sensors, instruments and connections," Madhavan reported. "Everything's in order. I've managed to restore limited power so we'll have a few more working stations and stable atmosphere. However, we are severely depleted on fuel. Even with extreme rationing we just don't have enough for more than a few days."

"We'll just have to tighten our belts then till we find a way out," Anara said, grimly. "You're sure there is no chance of getting the engines working?"

Madhavan shook his head. For the first time in many years, he was unable to explain an engineering problem. "The engines are in working order. We got them working. I just don't have enough fuel. We barely have any antimatter left. And, judging by what's outside or the lack of it, I don't think we'll find any matter here, let alone antimatter."

Anara turned to where she believed Ryan was standing in the engineering area. "Just what is outside, Ryan?"

Ryan was puzzled too. Madhavan and he had spent quite some time working over the conundrum. "I don't know how to describe this, except by calling it barren space or zero space if you like. I have no other information. Nothing we try seems to work. There is complete darkness. No reading of any kind on the limited sensors we have available. The cameras show absolute darkness, and I mean *absolute*. Even at the highest resolution and farthest focus, we have been unable to locate even one pinpoint of light."

"Zero space, huh?"

"Yeah. The absence of everything. No stars, no planets, no distant nebula, no light, nothing. Even gravity seems to be missing or very weak. The good part is that the lack of matter and gravity leads me to conclude that we are not inside the singularity. We seem to have passed through it completely."

"Meaning it was a wormhole. Well, well, looks like you were right, Manisha." Anara spread her arms and felt around her till she hit what felt like the back of a chair. She swung it around and sat down not realising that she was facing away from her team. Ryan,

Madhavan and Manisha dutifully and quietly walked around her so that they faced her again.

"But a portal to where?" continued Anara. "Don't get me wrong. I am happy we are in one piece, but I'd be happier if we were in one piece back on *Earth.*" *I wish I could see this phenomenon. Maybe I'd get a better idea. What a wondrous name—zero space. Damn these eyes.*

The door opened and Fraser walked in. "Sorry, I'm late but the doctor needed help keeping tabs on people who seem to be going out of their minds. The screaming is enough to wake the dead and the tranquilisers are not effective anymore."

"How many are affected, Colonel?"

"I counted fifteen so far including six of my troops. The Doc has not been able to isolate the cause of the illness."

"That is not good. That is not good. We need to get them to a proper hospital," said Anara, agitated. "That's what they need. A group of specialists who can figure out what's wrong with them."

"Dr Khan is one of the best there is in space medicine," said Ryan, "That's why he's here with us."

"Ryan, Dr Khan is top of his profession, but he's just one person. How can he help fifteen patients at the same time? Even with the help of the autobots? We need to find a way out so we can get our people the care they need, and fast."

"Could it be that our current region of space is affecting them?"

"Don't know enough yet to make a connection," said Ryan. "It could be the residual effects of the journey through the black hole and a fallout of the intense gravity fields. Our brains do work on electrical impulses, you know, and all that surging energy could've just fried the circuits. Sorry. I didn't mean to be impolite."

"Will you guys stop apologising to me every few minutes please? Please? I'm tired of you treating me like some sort of diseased person who is about to die. For the last time, I'm blind not incapacitated. Whatever has happened to me, I can deal with it, okay?" It came out harsher than intended, but she meant every word of it.

"Understood, Captain," Ryan said, about to apologise again and holding back in the nick of time.

She felt a little calmer. "Thank you. Now, let's get back to the problem at hand. "We may not have data to make an inference, but we can make some reasonable assumptions from whatever theories are available, right? First, let's look at the possibilities. Ryan?"

"Um. Of course," he started pacing slowly, putting his thoughts into words. "Picking up from our conversation just before we entered the black hole, we had advanced on the notion that the black hole serves as a gateway and we have found that to be true. I looked up some information. What I found are three probabilities." He moved to bring up a screen, then realising it would not work with the low levels of power; he pulled out a data tab. Stretching it open he laid it out on a table.

"I'll read as I write. Three possibilities—a different dimension, a baby universe, or a different location within our own universe."

"Wait. Wait. Wherever we are, isn't the easiest way out through our entrance? Why can't we just travel back the way through which we came in? Just reverse our course?"

"Uh. That would have been worth trying if we knew the location of the black hole from this side. Unfortunately, we have been drifting for some time. At least that is what I can deduce in the absence of any outside references. In any case, there is no indication or manifestation of the black hole anywhere near us. We're lost in zero space."

"If we could find it, would we be able go back through it?" asked Manisha.

"I've thought about it and it may not be feasible. Sure, we could reverse our graviton field again and manage to fly back, but once we do reach the other side, we would still be within the gravity well of the black hole and be sucked right back in. Then we would reverse fields again and be right back here, where we are right now. Ad infinitum."

"An endless loop," said Anara.

"Exactly. Besides, our current fuel reserves wouldn't allow us to make even one attempt let alone an infinite loop. But, let's come back to this a little later. Let's discuss another possibility—a wormhole."

"What's a wormhole?" asked the Colonel.

"Einstein-Rosen bridges," Anara responded, absently.

Fraser frowned in confusion. "How about plain English?"

"A wormhole's a hypothetical bridge between two widely separated regions of space-time, Colonel," Ryan said. "Kind of like a shortcut in space which can allow someone to travel vast distances in a very short time. Thought to be unstable, full of dangerous radiation or exotic matter."

This should become part of training in the JITF camp, thought Fraser with an inward sigh. To the others, he said, "That sounds rather like the black hole we came through, doesn't it?"

"Yes, it does. The only problem with this theory is that such wormholes are supposed to be bridges in space which can take us light years away, maybe even thousands of light years away but within *normal* space. We would still be able to observe stars and galaxies from wherever we were. Out here we clearly have nothing outside."

The door opened and an autobot nurse entered. Its mechanical voice was emotionless. "Captain Anara, you must come quickly. There is a crisis in Medical. Dr Khan has asked for you right away."

19

No Way Out

Medical was in uproar. Every single bed was occupied with strapped-down patients attempting to break free of their beds, all the while wailing in agony. A similar number of the crew were writhing on the floor, held down by whomever Dr Khan could spare.

"Oh my God!" cried Manisha, pulling Anara to one side so she wouldn't get hurt in the pandemonium.

"What is happening, Ryan? Find the doctor!" said Anara urgently.

Ryan nodded and disappeared into the bedlam. He was back within a very short time. "Manisha, you and the Colonel are needed here. Go help in any way you can. I'll brief the Captain and join you. Colonel, we need more of your troops. Summon them to Medical, please."

He guided Anara outside.

"This is bad. Whatever is afflicting the crew is getting worse. We have two dead crew persons, three are listed critical, and fifteen more are seriously affected. The doctor has still not been able to find the cause, leave alone a cure."

"It's this space or our journey through the black hole that's causing it, isn't it? What can I do to help?"

"There is nothing we can do here. Dr Khan is doing the best he can. JITF medics are already involved. I've asked for all available people to come down and be on standby, except for Madhavan, a couple of his engineers and you. You need to get to work to get us out of here. If this gets any worse, we may not have a crew left to save."

"But we have not even completed the theoretical discussions yet. How the hell am I supposed to save them if we do not have answers?"

"Murphy's Law will always be with us, won't it; whatever can go wrong will. I don't know the way out yet. I am needed here for some more time. You know everything there is to know. Keep working on a solution, Captain. Maybe you can find us a nugget to work on. I will see what the doctor needs and then join you, okay? I'll send someone to guide you back."

Anara cursed her helplessness as she waited in the corridor for an escort back to Ops. It was bad enough that she could not see but her inability to help her crew grated at her nerves the most. The deaths were on her head, of course. Her doubts threatened to overwhelm her again. Thankfully, the arrival of her escort broke her reverie and she allowed herself to be guided back to Ops.

***

I wonder how much time it will take before I get used to being blind. She felt her way around Ops, trying to remember the layout and familiarising herself with it. She wanted to be able to walk unaided around this one room at least. A soft ping alerted her that she was not alone.

"Hello, Captain."

"Narada, is that you? You're back! That's a relief."

"Yes. The backup computer has been restored and I have limited abilities available. I take it things have not gone well in my brief absence."

"Narada, I'm glad you're here. Yes, things are not going well. Two people are dead and there will be more if we cannot find a way out. I'll brief you."

"No need, Captain. I've brought myself up to speed over the last hour. Three people dead do not augur well for *Antariksh*."

"Two, not three, Narada," Anara corrected him.

"Sorry Captain, but crewmember Jas died a few minutes ago."

So much death. Anara broke down, shedding silent tears for her comrades and for herself. *How much longer can we hold on? I wish I could be stronger. I wish there was something more I could do. Some hope I could provide to those that remain.*

"Is everything all right, ma'am?"

She pulled herself together, wiping her eyes. This was not the time to grieve.

"I'm fine. We need to continue our research, you and I, till Ryan joins us. Put his notes up on the screen, will you."

"Here you go. All notes synchronized."

Which problem do I tackle first—the cause of the illness, or how to get out of our present predicament?

"Let's recap the three possibilities—wormhole, a different dimension and baby universe. What would be the manifestation of a different dimension, Narada? How would be perceive it?"

"The three dimensions of space—length, breadth and height along with the fourth dimension of linear time, are perceived readily by all humans. They constitute what we call spacetime. A continuum. They exist together. Our instruments are calibrated for these four dimension. The fifth or higher dimensions are postulated to be unobservable by humans and their instruments. They are possibly sub-atomic, even smaller than the smallest particles of matter we have observed till date."

"If we cannot observe more dimensions, then how do we know they even exist?"

"That is a matter of mathematics more than physics, though the two are invariably inter-related. Some of the solutions in physics, like string theory, or the Grand Theory can only be possible if we consider more than four dimensions. In fact, string theory needs ten dimensions to prove the theory itself. But again, we have no empirical evidence. As you know, we are still struggling to find the unification of gravity and quantum theory. Even the Grand Theory is not yet complete."

"Yeah, it is not possible to use gravity to describe what happens at the subatomic level any more than quantum theory can explain what happens at the cosmological scale." She sighed and slumped a bit. "In all these years, we have managed to achieve breakthroughs in breaking the light barrier, quantum entanglement and even in proving that dark matter exists, and yet..."

Anara pushed herself back in her chair. At least all this talk about scientific principles was allowing her to stow away the recent tragedies in a corner of her mind and look at them in an abstract manner. Reality would hit her soon but for the moment she could immerse herself in something other than death.

She thought hard. *Microscopic dimensions, smaller than the most fundamental particles.*

"Narada, what about the fundamental forces and gravity? Where do they fit into this multi-dimensional model?"

"At the simplest level it is believed that the reason gravity, exerted by graviton particles, can act over such large distances and yet be so weak is because the bulk of gravitons move through the fifth dimension."

Gravitons! Of course. That can be a connection. She sat up.

"Narada, in a black hole where matter is cramped into zero volume, theorise—can matter pass into the fifth dimension and gravitons escape into our four dimensions? What I'm saying is, is it possible matter is not really compressed to zero volume but exists in a different space altogether?"

"I do not have sufficient information to confirm your hypothesis, but it is a possibility, yes."

"Hold that thought. Let's get back to the third idea—baby universes. Describe their potential physical construct?"

"There are some theories postulated in the twenty-first century and reaffirmed in recent time. Baby universes are self-contained universes, which branch off from our own with possible similar properties. To grasp the concept, we must first understand the concept of imaginary time. Our 'real' time flows linearly but imaginary time flows at right angles to our time. If someone falls into a black hole, they may go off into a smaller universe or a baby universe. Time will continue to flow for them for years together but if they ever come back to normal space, they will find that only an instant has passed in normal space-time. Our universe is connected to baby universes through black holes and white holes."

"Hold on, hold on!" *The solution could not be as simple as white holes, could it?* "Refresh on white holes. They are supposed to be the theoretical opposite of black holes, aren't they? They cannot be entered from the outside, that is, from our normal universe."

"That is correct. Instead of attracting matter and energy from the outside, a white hole supposedly attracts antimatter and negative energy from the inside and *expels* normal particles and energy into normal space. A baby universe may have both black and white holes. With matter and energy going into a black hole and out of the white hole, the baby universe is able to maintain equilibrium and remain stable for any amount of time. Then, of course, there is Hawking radiation." Narada had more concepts up his sleeve.

This is too deep. Imaginary time? White holes? Hawking radiation? How can we ever stitch all of these concepts together to find a solution?

Her head was spinning. She needed to rest. *I'm just so tired. If I could only close my eyes for some time... Ryan. Yes, she and Ryan could make sense out this madness together. Yes. Ryan.*

She slept. A sleep full of dreams. She was one with the Universe again.

***

It seemed only seconds had passed when she was woken up by a gentle prodding.

"Who is it?" She was groggy. *Was it still night? Why didn't someone switch on the lights?* "Lights!" she called out. "Lights!"

"It's okay. It's okay. It's me. Ryan. You must've fallen asleep."

She ran her hand over her eyes. They were open. *I am blind. Blind. Better get used to it.*

"Sorry." She pushed herself up against the arm of her chair and sat up. *I can't even see what I look like right now.* She ran her hands through her hair and pushed it back into some semblance of order.

"I was going over some details with Narada and must've fallen asleep. I'm sorry. How long was I sleeping?" She was flustered. It had never happened before. *Shame on me for nodding off in the captain's chair.*

Ryan caught the fleeting look of pity that passed over Manisha's face and glared at her. He touched Anara's shoulder in sympathy. She let his hand lie there. Human contact felt good.

"I know. The notes are still on the screen and Narada has added to them. You were asleep for about half-an-hour, no more. Don't worry."

"How's the crew? Narada said there was one more death. Jas?"

"Yes. Jas didn't make it. And we lost one more—Krisha. She was part of the science team. Thankfully, we have not had any more new cases. Dr Khan has sedated the patients with the highest safe dosage. Any more, and he says their brain function will be severely affected."

"We have to do something!"

"And we are. We are trying to find the cause, and you and I are going to get us out of here. I promise." He needed to reassure her. *God knows what it feels like going blind suddenly, feeling helpless amidst all this chaos.* "Let's get back to work."

"I'm lost, Ryan. Five dimensions, white holes, baby universes? How can we connect all of that together? We only have theories to go on!"

"We do have theories and its time we put them to test," he said reassuringly. He needed her to focus. "It's all theoretical physics. Looks like you've covered all the possibilities. Narada, you have anything more to add?"

"No, Commander. There are some more impractical and unproven concepts with ten or even twenty-seven dimension solutions, but I do not believe any of those will help us in our current predicament except to enhance our knowledge of advanced mathematics. I will run them in the background just to rule out any possibilities. But with my reduced processing power it may take days before I can come back with any answers. We should consider Hawking radiation as well. The electromagnetic radiation released when a particle is absorbed by a black hole and its antiparticle pair is formed."

"Understood, but we are right now talking about the other side of a black hole. I'm not sure Hawking radiation fits into this right now," said Ryan as he reviewed the updated notes. To prove any of their hypotheses, they needed more data. He had a few ideas.

"Manisha, which scans of the outer space have you run so far?"

"Radar, sonar, and visual. Also, passive reading in various radio, audio and light frequencies—from infrared to ultraviolet. Zero feedback on all of them.

None of the more advanced instruments are working."

"Then we will use primitive science. Let's try a laser range probe. UV spectrum. Ten to the power twelve, one trillion kilowatts. Wide area sweep. Ten billionth of a second pulse."

"That will consume a lot of power, and we will only be able to scan maybe four or five AU in two hours, based on the speed of light. I mean, if I understand you correctly, you want to use the lasers as range finders or radar and see what they are reflected off. A laser pulse that can come back to us as a reflection within two hours. That means it should be strong enough to travel four or five AUs and reflect back to us while still strong enough for us to detect it." It made sense. With limited instruments and even limited power, it was a good option.

"Yep, you're right. So let's try it. Madhavan," he called out over the intercom, "we need power to the lasers. I've sent the data across."

Madhavan swiftly calculated the power reserves. "Whoa, commander. This is too much. It'll drain our reserves."

"Do it. My authority," instructed Anara.

"You're the boss," Madhavan said. "If you're sure. Ready in five."

"I've set the dispersion pattern and the receivers will be active throughout the test," confirmed Manisha.

"Acknowledged. Enable simultaneous reporting of any beam reflections. That will identify any objects near our position."

"Done."

"How will that help us?" asked Anara.

"We can use the reflected beams, if any, to form a rough model of the space around us. At the very least, it may provide us some reference points. If this is a baby universe, it might even be small enough for the beams to reflect off its boundary. It's just an experiment for now."

"Ok. But won't radar be enough for that purpose?"

"Not really. It's all about range. The beams I have sent out have a large aperture, short pulse and high energy. Their range will be much larger. Any reflection up to five AU will be sufficient for us to detect. That's about five times the distance from our Sun to Earth."

"Roger. Ready to fire laser pulses. One hundred seventy two points focused in a spherical grid," called out Manisha.

"Do it."

The pulses from the laser were only visible for a split second as they left the ship and disappeared into the void.

"What next while we wait?"

"Next we will explore the space around us with matter," Ryan said.

"Sorry?"

"I will shoot a bullet into the void, just beyond our electromagnetic screen and... uh... it will… it will…" He shook his head as if to drive away a pesky fly. "It will… show… antimatter… which…" He gripped his head. "Nooooooo…!"

20

Antimatter

"Commander! What's wrong?" Manisha ran to his side, trying to pull away his hands as he fell on the floor, writhing in agony. His body contorted and his eyes rolled up into his head.

"Nooooo…!" The screaming continued.

Anara too fell on her knees next to him, her hands searching to find his. "Call the doctor! Now, Manisha! Ryan? Ryan?"

Manisha tried to restrain the thrashing Commander, but he was too strong for her. "Get the doctor somebody!"

The screaming filled the room as Ryan continued to flail. He had turned pale and was sweating profusely. Anara held his shoulders while Manisha sat on his feet to keep him from hurting himself.

The door flew open.

"Oh no! Not you too, Commander," cried the doctor, rushing in. "Hold his arm while I sedate him!"

Anara felt and gripped his right arm tightly while the doctor administered a dermaspray. Ryan's body relaxed slowly in stages. His breath became sluggish.

"What happened to him?" Anara panted as she released her grip.

"The symptoms are the same. He's been afflicted just like the others. How did it happen?"

"One minute he was talking and then he started screaming and collapsed," Anara said, trying to keep the agitation from her voice. "Can you help him? We can't make this work without him."

"This is all I can do. The illness is spreading across the ship in stages. It's only a matter of time before all of us are affected. The sedatives do not help much, and I have already given him the maximum dose. If only I could induce a deeper sleep, we might stand a chance. But this sedative is all I've got. I'm sorry."

"I'm sick of hearing sorry!" Anara shouted. "Everyone today is sorry about something or the other. Well, we can either feel sorry or we can act! No more sorries!"

The doctor looked at her in alarm. By force of recent habit, he wondered if she was losing it too.

She turned towards the doctor's voice. "You said you need to induce sleep. You mean like a coma?"

Not sure where she was going with this, he thought before replying. "Not exactly. A medically induced coma can be very risky and will require artificial respiration using a ventilator. We only have a few of those and I cannot oversee everyone in this hazardous procedure even with automatons."

"What about our pods? Our capsules?"

"Pods?"

"The pods in our *dome*. They are designed to induce artificial sleep and we have enough for all our people and a few spare ones as well. And if we switch on the *dome* activating the cocoon, we can isolate the patients from outside space completely. Will that help?" Anara was clutching at straws.

The doctor considered. "I don't know if it will, but I have no other ideas at hand. If it is something in our vicinity or environment which is affecting them, it may work. There is no harm in trying, for sure."

"Let's go then! Help me lift him up. C'mon!" She attempted to lift Ryan's feet.

"Captain, you can't do this. Let me. Fireman's carry, doc. Help me out."

Manisha hunched down at the knees while the doctor laid Ryan on his back. She bent Ryan's legs, pulled his left arm upwards and swung him across her shoulders. She ran out of the room managing the heavy weight on her shoulder quite easily and the doctor followed her. Anara was left behind again.

"Narada, get me the Colonel."

Narada placed the call.

"Colonel, Ryan has collapsed as well, but we may have a solution to save the crew. I want you to get the patients into the *dome.* We will place them in stasis and light up the cocoon. The doctor is there already. I'll meet you there. Please hurry!"

"On my way!"

"One more thing, I need a robo-soldier as a guide. I can't keep pulling people off their duties to be my guide. A robot will be sufficient for my needs."

"Done. Someone will be with you shortly. Fraser out." He rose to do her bidding, his respect for her growing manifold by the minute.

This is one strong woman. Her crew is dying around her, her first officer may be dying as well, and she herself is blind. Yet, she is still running strong.

"Narada, call Madhavan," Anara instructed next.

When she was connected, she said, "Madhavan, we need the *dome* operational with at least twenty pods. Get a team there."

"*Dome*? Are we going to light speed?"

"No. It's a medical experiment. It may help save the rest of the crew. Get it done!"

"Hold on, Captain. I'm not sure we will have enough power to spare for the *dome*! I'm barely able to hold the engines together and just a few minutes ago, we sent out lasers at a trillion kilowatts. One hundred and seventy-two beams. We will exhaust the fuel in days!"

"Madhavan, if we don't save the crew there will be no use for all the fuel we manage to save anyway" *No fuel. No crew. Antariksh would be lifeless and adrift.* "How many days of fuel do you have at the current rate of consumption?"

"Ten days, give or take one or two."

"And with the *dome* functioning?"

"I'll need to check."

"Rough cut is good enough for now."

"Uh," he hesitated, doing the mental arithmetic, "maybe forty, forty-five hours. Two days tops."

Two days to find our way out. It isn't going to happen. At least if the laser beams find an object and reflect back; I might get some leads.

"Do it," she ordered.

"Yes, ma'am," he said, resignedly. *No one listens to me any longer. If I can figure out how we lost the fuel, it might just be possible to prevent further leakage. We should find a way to carry space cans of antimatter. Even a few hundred grams. Then I could refuel the ship whenever required. Now that's a thought I can work on; portable antimatter containers.* Madhavan shook his head.

***

A light hum filled the corridor indicating that the *dome* was functioning. A small crowd was gathered outside the entrance when Anara arrived, guided by a robot-soldier.

"Doc?"

"It seems to be working, Captain," he replied, exultant. "The patients are stable. That was one hell of an idea!"

"A calculated hunch, doctor. At least we have bought ourselves some time. All of forty hours. I want you to gather all non-essential personnel and place them inside the pods as well. We don't know how and why this region of space alters the human brain, so we must try and protect our people as best as we can. You, me, the Colonel, Madhavan, Manisha—we will get to work. Manisha, ask Madhavan to get the rest of the pods operational. He's also to pick two of his best people to work with him. Tell him to ask for volunteers. People should be able to choose if they are ready to face the prospect of falling violently ill. Colonel, we need a few troops to help us. Plus one nurse with the doctor. Only one nurse, mind you. No more than a dozen people overall. Understood?"

"Yes," they all murmured.

"Let's get to work. The clock is ticking. Manisha, Colonel—you're with me." She turned and found the robot-soldier's hand. "Take me to Ops, please."

The robot acknowledged her order and led her down the corridor.

"What's your name?" she asked.

"My designation is S12. Robot platoon 35," it replied as they climbed the stairs.

"Thank you, S12." *Why am I thanking a robot?*

"It's my duty, Captain."

***

Several minutes later, with most of the crew in stasis, Anara sat in Ops with Manisha and Fraser. *This game needs to be played to its logical end.* "Narada, any feedback on the laser detectors?"

"None so far. I am monitoring them continuously."

"Right, right. Suggestions?"

"What did Commander Ryan mean by firing a bullet? He said something about antimatter." The Colonel was looking for a part to play. He could fire a bullet.

"Particle anti-particle pairs are postulated to be created at the event horizon of black holes. One of them may be absorbed and the other one is emitted causing what is known as Hawking Radiation. So, when normal matter is absorbed, an anti-particle is also created at the event horizon," replied Narada.

Anara sat down in her chair. *Particle-antiparticle pair created at black hole. Anti-particles exit the event horizon. So, at a white hole, the opposite must happen. An antiparticle-particle pair is created; the antiparticle remains inside the event horizon, or inside the white hole, while the corresponding normal particle is emitted into normal space. Does this mean matter entering a black hole stays at the singularity and the corresponding anti-particles enter the fifth dimension or baby universe?*

She spoke her thoughts out loud.

"It is theoretically possible, but like I'd said there is no empirical evidence for the same," observed Narada.

"Till now. That is what Ryan was trying to prove by firing a bullet!" *Wow! That's genius level thinking!*

"What bullet?" Manisha was getting confused.

"Anti-particles are opposite of normal matter. So, a negatively charged electron will have a positron—same mass opposite charge. A neutron will have an anti-neutron. If the two types of particles meet, they annihilate themselves in a huge burst of energy. This matter-antimatter explosion under control is what we use to power our ship."

Manisha nodded, catching on. "You mean, if we are surrounded by anti-particles and we fire a bullet outside, it will cause an explosion?"

"Yes. That's the only way we can determine the presence of anti-particles. Rough and dirty. Our sensors are barely functional. Our own anti-matter detectors in the engine room have very limited range and it would take too long to modify them. So Ryan thought of the bullet."

"But if we have antiparticles outside, why haven't *we* been destroyed so far? We are made of matter, aren't we? Hundreds of tons of matter, in fact. Or is that a stupid question?" asked Fraser.

"No. It's not a stupid question at all. The reason could be the strong electromagnetic field surrounding the ship. It is designed to help deflect space dust that can rupture our hull. It is always functional even when we are standing still. Electromagnetism is also what we also use to keep matter-antimatter separate till required for the energy reaction. In a way that EM field surrounding our ship has been protecting us. Ryan is truly a genius. He figured out a way to help us observe anti-matter even when we have no functional sensors. The EM field focusses outwards so a bullet will get through just like our missiles."

"So, we fire a bullet and prove his theory? That's it?" That Fraser could do.

"Yes, that's exactly what we do, and you may be a co-winner of the Nobel, Colonel!" Anara said, with a broad grin. They would at least have one breakthrough if the bullet caused an explosion as soon as it exited the EM field.

"Get set then. Get a long-range rifle with a single bullet. I assume you will be the one doing the honours?" Progress, however small, improved her mood considerably.

I will beat you yet, she challenged the black hole in her mind.

21

A Long Shot

The Colonel stood inside the airlock waiting for it to open. He was clad in an EVA suit, connected with a tether. In his hand, he held a Barrett 105AI. The AI-supported, long-range sniper rifle felt good in his hands. He had just one bullet in the chamber. He had taken some time deciding which gun and bullet combination to use. He needed the longest possible range, which meant he had to use a sniper rifle like the Barrett. The bullet had to be as light as possible so it could travel the distance to cross the EM barrier and yet not have any more than the bare minimum mass. He had finally chosen a 150–grain cartridge and filed it to reduce the weight to less than one gram. If the theory was right, it would be enough to cause an immense matter-antimatter explosion and yet not damage the EM screen. 150–grain was the least he required if he wanted to achieve the required range. He did not need the video-scope because there was no specific target to be shot. This would be the easiest shot of his life, but possibly also the deadliest.

Major Kevin stood ready to activate the outer door, waiting for the signal from Ops.

"You sure you don't want me to do this, sir? It's my job after all." Kevin knew the answer, but he had to offer. To be truthful, he was a little jealous that he would not be doing the shooting.

His boss shook his head. "Not a bloody chance, Major. It's my shot today."

Kevin nodded, gave a thumbs up to the Colonel and closed the inner door.

"We're ready, Captain. Colonel Fraser is in place."

"Roger, Major. Madhavan, status?" asked Anara.

"Integrity of the EM field is stable. Range extended to five hundred metres. Power diverted to port side EM emitters to reinforce the field."

"All right then. Manisha, give permission to proceed. Brace for impact."

"It's a go, Major," Manisha informed Kevin.

"Roger that. Best of luck, sir." He waited, then opened the airlock. He had to give his boss exactly two seconds before he closed the door again. An open door would leave the ship vulnerable during the explosion.

The Colonel was prepared. The rifle was already in his hands, the butt nestling comfortably on his shoulder. No sooner had the door opened than he fired, brought the barrel down, threw away the rifle, turned around and lay down flat on the floor with his hands on his head. The door closed behind him just as the darkness beyond was torn apart by a massive detonation.

***

There was no sound, just a burst of energy bright enough to turn the blackness into day for a few seconds before the light dissipated. The shockwave was not as intense as expected because the anti-particle density was low. Bursts of energy collided with the electromagnetic screen, lighting it up in a spectacular display of fireworks. Luckily, the screen held but the ship rocked violently. The explosions propagated away from the ship as anti-matter particles further away were consumed.

Not able to visualise what was happening outside, the few crewmembers on board, held on tight to their seats and the restraints, waiting for the jolting to cease.

***

The first shockwave passed, then another and another. It took time but the explosions finally dissipated as all matter in the bullet was annihilated, and the ship grew still. Fraser lifted himself off the floor. He walked to the inner door and waited. Major Kevin opened it and helped him out of the airlock.

"That was quite dramatic, wasn't it, Major?"

"That it was, sir. Good shooting, by the way. Back to Ops?"

***

"Passive detector readings are coming in now. Matter-antimatter annihilation confirmed, ma'am. The Commander was right. We are in a field of antimatter."

"What's the particle density?"

"It's quite low. Only around five thousand per cubic centimetre. That's surprising considering the size of the explosion, isn't it?" Manisha remarked.

"Narada?"

"Not just one explosion. It was a series of explosions but with a difference so minute even our sensors were not able to read them. The first contact of matter caused a chain reaction which progressed rapidly in thousandths of a second. Presence of antimatter is confirmed. Particle density here is twice that of matter in normal interstellar space in our own universe. I am unable to find an explanation for the difference. How would you like to proceed?"

"I'm not sure. I was so caught up in trying out the experiment; I did not wait to think what we would do with this data. At least the EM screen held. Connect me to Engineering." A chirp announced an active connection. "Madhavan, how're things down there?" asked Anara.

"We are holding together. The shields took out more energy than I had provided for. I estimate we are now down to twelve hours of antimatter fuel."

Manisha chipped in. "But we are surrounded by antimatter! Can't we just collect what we need?"

Madhavan sighed. "And just how do we do that? Using a scoop? Get real, Lieutenant." He was too tired to care if he was being rude to another officer. Manisha looked sheepish. Anara frowned, but chose to ignore the outburst too. "Anyway," Madhavan continued, "the density is too low. Even if I could design and deploy a magnetic field to form a... a funnel, the few specks of antimatter we do manage to gather would not be enough for our needs. Not to forget, I need pure antimatter particles of a single type exactly opposite to our stored matter particles. One hundred percent pure, Captain. That's why we manufacture and store antimatter one particle at a time. Do you have any idea what type of particles are outside or their purity?"

"Uh no. We only know it is antimatter based on the last test," said Anara.

"There you go. It is rocket science. You can't just pick up what you need by the roadside and expect it to work. One speck of contamination in our fuel and the unbalanced explosion will spread *our* particles throughout the galaxy!"

"Alright. Alright. Understood, Madhavan. Calm down. We can't use the particles. Anara out." She sat brooding for some time. "What about the readouts from the lasers we have sent out, Manisha? We should have had some observations. It's been some time."

"No reflections detected so far. The lasers must not have hit anything. That may or may not mean there are no solid objects out there. It was a long shot anyway. We only fired a hundred and seventy-two beams. That didn't even cover all degrees on a plane, forget about covering all the degrees of a sphere."

Anara removed her restraint and stood up. She wanted to walk. It always helped her think. That was getting difficult: both walking and thinking. *Twelve hours. That is all I have to save my crew and my ship.*

"If there are antimatter particles out there, where have they come from? Spontaneous generation? Leftovers from a big bang event?" wondered Anara.

"What came first, this space or these particles? Narada?"

"As I had stated earlier, it is more likely they are the antiparticle equivalents of matter absorbed by a black hole," stated Narada. "Maybe it is Hawking radiation in reverse. Some of the antiparticles escape at the event horizon but a lot more get passed on to another dimension."

"Which then turn into particles at the white hole and flow back into our universe. So there should be a flow, shouldn't there? From the black hole to the white?"

"Flow? What kind of flow, ma'am?" Manisha was quite involved now.

"A flow of particles, Manisha! Like... like a river, though of extremely low density. We need to find the direction of flow and follow it to reach the white hole."

"And then what?"

Anara did not have the answer yet to that, but there was a glimmer of an idea. "Let's cross that bridge when we come to it. I'm hoping we will be able to find a reverse portal to get out of this space—a white hole. Narada, anything we can use to detect the flow of particles?"

"With only five thousand particles of antimatter every cubic centimetre? Our detectors are not powerful enough to monitor them."

"We can use the detectors from our matter-antimatter engines, but they would need to be outside our EM screen to work properly. Only, once they are outside the screen they will be annihilated on coming in contact with the antimatter. That would probably destroy us as well." *A classic catch-22. Damned if I do. Damned if I don't.*

"Madhavan get up here. I've got another task for you."

***

Madhavan walked through the darkened corridors, a breathing mask on his face. He shivered in the cold. With environment controls down, temperatures across the ship had plummeted. Only three areas, besides the dome, had heat, light and air—Ops, Medical and Engineering. The whole situation felt like his worst nightmare. Give him an engine to work with, a mechanical problem to solve, and he was in his element. Being captured by a black hole was definitely not his cup of tea. Still he was grateful to be alive and safe from whatever was killing his crewmates. He half-walked, half-staggered into Ops, exhausted from having been at his station without a break for several hours.

"Hey, Captain. How're you holding up?" He tried to sound cheerful.

Anara turned around at the sound of his voice.

"I'm fine, Madhavan. And you?" Her voice was kindly. Madhavan had become another one of her rocks. Solid, dependable.

"I can manage, though a few hours of sleep and a decent cup of coffee would work wonders. I must tell you, this has been one hell of a ride. I can't wait to find what else you've got in store for me. We've got less than twelve hours of juice left. The ship took a real beating with the last test. What have you planned next for me?"

"Another conundrum which is right down your alley. It involves detecting antimatter flow in the space outside. That's why I called you up here. Is there anything that you can rig up?"

"An antimatter detector? Sure. I can bring up a couple from the M-AM fuel chamber. Where do you want them?"

"The antimatter particles are outside our EM screen. Five thousand particles per cubic centimetre."

"Outside the screen? You mean out there?" He walked over to a porthole and stared outside. "But if there are antimatter particles out there, the matter in the detectors will annihilate when it comes in contact with them. I explained all this earlier." He turned around looking at her quizzically. "Isn't that what happened when you fired the bullet? Wasn't that the point of the whole exercise?"

"It was and we proved our assumption. Now we need to take the next step. With Ryan out of action, I'm really trying to improvise." Was it her imagination or was the air in Ops starting to taste stale? Twelve hours of power remaining. Madhavan must have used up all his ingenuity trying to squeeze out every bit of energy from the system. "Can't you rig the detectors up with some sort of a portable EM shield or something?"

While Madhavan was considering the possibilities, the door opened and the Colonel walked in adorned with his own breathing apparatus.

"Maybe," Madhavan said. "But I have very little time to design, build and put up a portable EM generator of sufficient strength. Can't be done. Besides, with a portable shield, the detectors won't work. They detect particles based on changes in the magnetic field they generate, when it encounters antimatter particles. With another EM shield around the detector, there is no way they can work." He shook his head. "Sorry. But you'll need another idea."

Anara walked up to the sound of his voice, reached out and held his arms. "I don't have any other ideas. I don't even know what we will do after we detect the flow, but it was a working hypothesis. Without a detector, we have nothing."

***

"Looks like my excellent shot did not have the consequences you expected, Captain," remarked Fraser.

"S12, come here," Anara commanded. The robot moved to her side and she walked a few metres towards the Colonel with its support.

"Yes, it did. It allowed us to definitively prove the existence of antimatter outside. Let's not give up hope so easily." She turned around, her eyes bright and alert though without sight. "We have faced multiple hurdles in the last few days and yet we have survived. The universe has thrown its greatest challenge at us and we have survived. We have faced the ultimate form of death known to humankind, and yet with some skill, a few timely hunches and a bit of luck we have cheated it. I have been on the verge of giving up so many times and yet we have persisted. Isn't that what human spirit is all about? Tenacity and belief that there is always a way! This time I am sure we will find a way. We have to believe, and we have to try, if not for ourselves then for our colleagues who are in stasis and dependant on us for safety." *It is always about balancing energy, isn't it? Even with people. It is my job to counter the negative energy in my people with positivity. How could I have missed that?*

Her small speech had added positive energy to her crew. It held them together. Held her together.

"Well? Do you wanna keep trying or throw your hands up and give up?" She threw down the challenge to her team.

No one spoke for a moment.

"We will try, of course, till, as you so neatly put it, the universe manages to crush us. Tell me what I can do," said Fraser. This woman was a great officer. He was proud to be working with her. He had finally understood Captain Anara, the individual. The leader.

"We keep trying to make some sense of this new universe around us and use Narada to replace Ryan. He's good, of course, and he can process billions of calculations per second. But he cannot think out of the box like Ryan could. No offence, Narada."

"None taken, ma'am. What would you like to discuss?"

"We are not able to detect either of the holes, right—the black hole through which we entered this space or the theoretically possible white hole we are seeking? But we have also not left our position ever since we came in. Maybe what our sensors have missed, our eyes will show us. Your eyes I mean. We need to travel."

"I'm not sure what you're proposing? Could you be more specific for me to program a route?" If he had been human, Narada would have cocked his head to one side, listening intently.

"If the lasers do not come back, if we cannot see the antiparticles, then we need to search the space around us using our own eyes. We move the ship and take a look," said Anara.

"You want to fly the ship into the void surrounding us? With no means of navigation, minimal propulsion and the four of us as the crew? That's…that's…" Madhavan was at a loss for a diplomatic word.

"Crazy, right?" Anara cut in, with a grin. "On the other hand, why do we need navigation? There is nothing out there! At sub-light speed, we will not run into anything, even though I am hoping we do. How long can we sustain sub-light speed, say at twenty percent?"

"You're serious, aren't you? You do know that even for twenty percent sub-light speed we will need fuel. Lots of it. Fuel that we don't have. We can't make the ship go to those speeds."

"How about a hundred thousand kph? Is that possible?" Anara was persistent.

Madhavan thought this through. "I know I promised to help you any way I can, but you keep asking me to perform miracles." Equations and numbers churned in the back of his mind.

"We have had quite a few miracles, Mr Madhavan. What's the harm in seeking a few more?" Fraser said. "It is clear that she is serious. Come, I'll help you, as will Major Kevin. Let's get started."

Madhavan gave him the eye, then grudgingly donned his breathing mask and followed Fraser out. He paused at the door and looked at Anara. "You can have two hundred thousand kph, not one. For two hours tops, no more." *It would be close, but I think we can pull this off. Just need to keep a sharp eye for any consumption spikes. What other equipment can I turn off to buy more time?*

"Thank you, Madhavan," she called to his retreating back as the door closed behind him and the Colonel.

***

"We have power," reported Manisha.

"The conn is yours, Manisha," The ship was in the hands of this young pilot now.

"Which way should we go?" Manisha asked.

"How about straight ahead? Easiest thing to do. You do realise we are never coming back here again, don't you? We can't drop a marker as a beacon because it will be immediately destroyed. And while we may be able to keep tabs on the distance we travel using inertial guidance, we will never know if we go off course. So straight line it is." *Amazing how much clarity a little bit of hope can give you.*

"Yes, ma'am," Manisha replied as the power display showed the engines ready to engage. She moved her hand to get the ship moving. "Increasing to two hundred thousand kph." The increasing vibrations filled her with a sense of familiarity. Flying a ship was what she had been trained to do.

22

The Flow

"All systems are failing, *Capitaine!* We cannot break the hold of the gravity."

"*Maudit!* Black hole!" That is what Captain Antoine's science officer had told him, but he could still barely believe it. Caught in the event horizon of a black hole! How could that have happened! For the past many hours, he had maintained maximum reverse thrust on his engines, but it had not worked. They were being in sucked in. They were out of time.

"Anyone has any more ideas, I am listening?" He paused. "*Antariksh.* They were in the same region as us. Maybe they have an answer?"

"We tried calling them, as you ordered, *Capitaine,*" Elise said. "They did not respond."

"Then no one is coming to our rescue. Marcel!" he called out to his engineer, "one last try. Reverse gravity now!"

The engineer was scrambling to carry out this command when the ship accelerated in the final stages. It was too little too late. The *CDG* with its crew had barely entered the singularity when the engines failed and the ship's gravity field collapsed.

***

Time passed in silence: only the soft whooshing of air from the circulation system could be heard in Ops. Anara had tilted her head back on the headrest and fallen into a light sleep.

"Captain! Captain! Wake up!" Manisha called out suddenly from her control station.

Anara was up instantly. *Wow! I fell asleep with my eyes open. A small advantage of being completely blind,* she thought sarcastically.

"I'm up, Manisha!" The most ridiculous thought hit her. "How did you know I was sleeping? I thought my eyes were open."

"They were, but you were snoring," she smiled. "Just a little." Manisha didn't mention she had used the opportunity to sneak off for a quick moment with Kevin in the corridor outside Ops. It had felt awesome, that stolen kiss and a hug in the midst of all this chaos, like they were cocking a snook at the dire circumstances they were in. She had never felt more alive.

Anara grunted. "My apologies. I don't seem to have control over this sleep. How far have we travelled? Have you found something?"

"I'm not sure. Time and speed calculations indicate we have travelled 45,000 kilometres. Narada is running an analysis of our camera footage. We observed a flash of light. It was momentary. It might have been glitch in the vision system, or I might even have imagined it, but I thought you'd like to know."

"You did not imagine it, Lieutenant. It was a burst of light. I have checked, the camera systems are working at optimum resolutions," reported Narada. "I estimate the distance to the phenomenon to be approximately seventy-five thousand kilometres."

"A flash of light?"

"Yes, a very brief flash, but it was there."

"Then let's get to it. Plot a course." She felt around for the communications control and failing to find it yet again, she asked Narada to connect her to Engineering.

"Madhavan, we might have something. I need the power for some more time."

"Captain, we are literally running on fumes."

"Something? *Anything*. Buy me some time."

"Another hour," Madhavan capitulated. "No more than that, please. Though I might have some good news. I have found a way to channel our EM field. We might be able to collect some antimatter. However, I need the ship to be perfectly still and the concentration of particles to be at least fifty thousand per cubic centimetre. Let me know if you find some, will you, ma'am?"

"Highly unlikely, Madhavan, but I will keep it in mind." She couldn't help smiling at his request. *Find me some antimatter, indeed.* "Narada, keep the intercom to Engineering open at all times. He needs to hear our every move and respond without wasting time waiting for instructions." Narada acknowledged the command.

"We are moving forward, though it will take at least another twenty minutes to reach the place," Manisha reported.

There was silence for some time. Then, Manisha exclaimed excitedly. "There! Another flash. Did you see that?"

"Yes, Lieutenant," acknowledged Narada. "A second flash. Much clearer than before. I estimate its distance to be less than fifty thousand kilometres."

"Theorise, Narada. What can it be?" instructed Anara.

"Based on the fact that there are antimatter particles in this space, and the explosion proceeded like a chain reaction very similar to our own experiment earlier, I would conclude that the flash was caused either by matter entering our baby universe and annihilating in contact with the antimatter, or it can be antimatter particles moving at relativistic speeds giving off photons as they lose energy and slow down."

"As they would if they were exiting a black hole! Brilliant! Narada, theorise again. Why are we able to see this now and not earlier?" There was no time to lose.

Narada had multiple options worked out in the background. "Two possibilities, Captain. One, we were simply facing the wrong direction and were too far away. Or two, the amount of matter absorbed by the black hole has suddenly seen a dramatic increase."

"Explanation?"

"Something big just came in through the black hole, possibly in a manner similar to ours, because the object did not join the mass at the singularity. Instead, it disintegrated part way through. The matter of the object collided with antimatter in phases." Narada was becoming more and more certain of his findings. They had more visual data than ever before.

"Sounds reasonable, right guys? And there was only one other object behind us in that region of space. We forgot all about the French ship. This may be them entering our space," observed Anara.

"The *CDG*! Let's find them. Maybe we can end up helping each other!" exclaimed Manisha.

23

One-Way Trip

"Captain, the flashes of light are most likely explosions. Whatever object that was, the *CDG* or something else, it has been destroyed." Narada reported.

Anara did not give up hope. Even a dead ship could help *Antariksh*. She would pray to God to rest the souls of the *CDG's* crew, but right now she had her own people to save.

"How much further do we have to go, Manisha?"

"Twenty thousand kilometres, ma'am. Narada, set up a countdown for every thousand kilometres."

"Done." A voice counted down the distance in the background.

"Also, display video on main holo."

The holo came alive.

"Any more flashes?" asked Anara.

"None so far," Manisha replied. She paused, then looked up perplexed at the reading she saw on her screen. "Narada, are you seeing this?"

"Yes I am. Let me try for a higher resolution."

"Ten thousand kilometres." The countdown continued.

"What is it?"

"It's difficult to make out the details, but there are multiple objects ahead. Whoa!"

"*What?*" cried out Anara.

"Multiple flashes. Distance approximately five thousand kilometres."

Antariksh lurched violently catching Anara off guard. The auto-activated safety belt kept her from falling, but she was sharply pulled back in her chair.

"More explosions. Intensity is increasing," Manisha kept calling out the visual images. "We cannot survive them with the present state of our shields. We need to keep our distance. All stop!" The AI took control and brought *Antariksh* to a halt.

"Five thousand five hundred kilometres," Narada reported.

"Reverse engines!" shouted Anara. That seemed to be the prudent thing to do. She cursed her blindness again for slowing her down.

Antariksh moved backwards.

"Ten thousand kilometres." The intensity of the explosions decreased but the ship continued to be jolted by shockwaves.

Madhavan rushed from station to station trying to keep the ship functioning against the repeated assaults. "Captain! What is happening? The screen took a huge hit. It could barely absorb the last explosion. One more like that and it will fail."

"Stand by, Madhavan. Manisha?"

"We are being battered by some sort of highly energised particles. The electromagnetic screens is repelling most of them or absorbing the impact of their energy. That's all I can make out from what I see on my screen. The initial explosions we encountered were massive, but they've significantly decreased in intensity...Wait..."

"What now? Manisha, you have to keep describing the scene to me."

"Yes, yes. Now I can see are multiple luminous trails of light."

"What do they look like? Tell me."

"Like fireworks in the sky! So many colours. And they keep blinking in and out."

"Those are highly energised standard subatomic particles moving at or near the speed of light," agreed Narada. "The explosions were probably the result of matter-antimatter annihilation. The Lieutenant is right. Some of these bursts are the particles impacting our EM screen."

"Are none of our sensors working now, Narada?"

"None that can detect antiparticles."

"Can you at least make out where the particles are coming from? Can we trace them to the entry point into our universe? That would lead us to the black hole, won't it?"

"Captain?" Madhavan was calling her again.

"Sorry. Yes, Madhavan?"

"Whatever you're planning to do, I implore you, don't take the ship into the chaos outside. The screen cannot hold out much longer."

"But that may be our way out! We need to get to the singularity. It can pull us back into our own normal universe."

"We will never survive past even a few kilometres in that sea of particles. Not even a few. Please. You must understand."

"Madhavan, if we miss this chance, with the amount of time available, we will die a cold death."

"Captain, even if I could give you enough power to get to the black hole, how will we ever generate the reverse gravitons to get through it? Why can't you understand?"

"What you cannot understand, Madhavan, is that there are ninety-six people on this ship whose lives depend on us getting out of here! What would you have me do if not try?" *What a choice in front of me—death by asphyxiation in the deathly cold of space when power runs out, or a mercifully fast death by riding into an ocean of antimatter without the protection of an electromagnetic screen.* "Like I said earlier, one step at a time. We have found our entry point. We will try and get into the black hole from this side. The alternative is to die here. Quite frankly I prefer taking my chances with a beast we defeated once before."

No one spoke up. *It is going to be my decision. This will probably—no, certainly—lead us into a violent death. Madhavan is right, it is a bad choice. We have already thought this through earlier. Even if we get through, we will be pulled back into the black hole. The infinite loop that Ryan was talking about. No. That is not the way. But isn't there something else we are missing?*

She took a deep breath. "You're right, Madhavan. I wasn't thinking straight. We can't go back, but we still have the white hole?"

"What white hole, ma'am?" Manisha was lost.

"You remember, we worked out that there is a white hole exiting a baby universe and the only way to find it may be by following the flow of particles? Well, didn't you just say, Manisha that we have streaks of light outside? Won't that indicate the paths being followed by the particles of antimatter?"

"It might," agreed Narada, trying to work out where she was going with this line of thought.

"We were not able to detect the flow so far because the detectors we have cannot be placed in the antimatter field. And now? Now we have a field of energised particles out there practically showing us the way! It's a fully lighted highway! It's our way out!"

"Captain, I must warn you." Narada had started working on some simulations with the available parameters. The results were not encouraging. "We may be able to locate the theoretical white hole, but we do not know how far it is from our position nor is there is any guarantee it will lead us out of here. My analysis shows that there is only a twenty-two percent chance that we will find it."

Anara sighed. "I know I can't see anything and yet I am asking you to take my word for it... but does any of you have a better idea?" She paused for an answer. "No? You, Madhavan? No? If we have no alternative, then I say we follow this path." She pulled off her restraints and staggered to her feet. "However. I can't ask all of you to put your faith in a blind woman's instinct, so what say we have a vote? Narada, can you ask the Colonel, Kevin and the medical team to come up here as well? They need to weigh in here. Fine with you guys?"

They nodded, then Manisha spoke up. "Sounds fair to me, though you know I will follow you come what may. You have gotten us this far. I am sure you will get us out of here."

"Thank you for the vote of confidence." It felt good that someone still believed in her.

"Me too, Captain," Madhavan put in. "Just one thing though, at the cost of sounding negative and repetitious. We can only make one trip. Towards what we can see in front of us even though it may destroy us in an instant or, towards that white hole which is so far only hypothetical. Either way it is going to be a one-way trip."

24

Yin And Yang

The seven people and one AI awake on the ship assembled in Ops. Anara sensed them gathering around her.

Will this be the last time we will be together? Alive that is.

"Before we get on with the vote, I want to thank each of you for your extraordinary courage and patience even though this is one journey I would not like to undertake again."

Madhavan found her blind eyes unsettling as they swept the room, open yet unfocussed.

"I have even lost count of the number of hours or days we have spent in this place. At any rate—and it seems I have been repeating this far too many times in the last few days—we have a choice to make." She ran a hand over her tired face. "We are down to the last hour of fuel, and we have to choose one of two paths ahead. Like I said it is only fair all of you get to participate in this choice."

"What about the people in stasis? Who speaks for them?" asked the Doctor.

"The burden of leadership will be ours, Doctor. Our decision will be binding on those who are absent and mute. We must act swiftly. Both the choices are perilous. Do we go towards the black hole, or the white? There is no way of knowing which choice is correct. Narada, you want to elaborate further?"

"The probable entrance to the black hole is surrounded by a field of antimatter. Our EM screen may not withstand the explosions which are still taking place. It is also not known if we will be able to enter the black hole from this side or if doing so will lead us to our normal universe or to another baby universe. On the other hand, the existence of a white hole, another possible exit route, is theoretical. It may or may not exist. The distance to such a white hole is also unknown. However, if we *can* reach it, it is most likely to provide us with a navigable route home. Based on all known theories, of course."

"Any questions, people?" Anara asked.

"I thought we would find the *Charles de Gaulle*," Fraser said. "Where is that ship?" *The poor sods.*

"In all probability these antimatter particles and the explosions we encountered are all that remains of the *CDG,* if it was the *CDG* at all. That ship was smaller and is unlikely to have survived the entry into the singularity."

"Nor did it have the exemplary crew of *Antariksh* on board. Anyway, I believe the white hole is our best chance given our fuel status. My vote is for the white hole," declared Madhavan.

"What about harvesting some antimatter from what is outside?" asked Kevin.

"I checked up on that. I can collect enough particles, but I do not know the type of these particles outside. Matter-antimatter reactions require the particles to be mixed in precise masses. If the particles outside are antiprotons and I try to make them work with our positrons, we will get unequal, or worse, uncontrolled reaction rates. And I won't have any way of knowing about the particles till I get them onboard. Just the process of collection will take several hours. We will run out of fuel much before that."

"So even if we manage to cross the barrier, we will still have no fuel left to travel back home. We can still die in normal space from an empty fuel tank, can't we?" asked Manisha.

"Not necessarily. I can continue to use our fusion drives. It will be way slower, but it will get us close enough to Earth to send a signal and wait for rescue," answered Madhavan.

Anara allowed herself a brief moment to contemplate the one thing they were all ignoring for now.

We may get to Earth only to be swallowed by the black hole when it consumes our entire solar system. We are only buying time. Can a whole solar system fit into this baby universe? What a fascinating thought. How big is this zero space anyway?

"One thing at a time," she said, more to herself than the others. "We need to decide now. Show of hands?"

Five hands rose, almost in unison. Everyone looked at the two JITF officers, who stood with their hands by their sides.

"Narada, what's the count?"

"Five to two, ma'am. The Colonel and Major Kevin are not in favour."

She gave a small sigh of relief. It was an acceptable ratio.

"It is all right, Colonel. None of us will hold this against you."

"You misunderstand me, Captain Anara. I may not understand much of the science that you people have been discussing, but I understand you. I understand your drive to succeed. I understand your loyalty to your people. I understand that you have kept us alive despite all the obstacles we have faced. I trust you as a leader. Major Kevin and I will follow your lead."

And with that their bond was sealed. Anara bowed her head in acknowledgement.

"Then it is settled. We proceed towards the white hole. Manisha, maximum possible speed ahead. Madhavan, can we continue with two hundred thousand kph?"

"Yes. I will fire up the fusion reactors. I'll link them to the *dome*. Even if the M-AM drive fails, it will keep the people alive for some more time."

"No," replied Anara as the ship eased forward and reached its peak velocity. "We will have to turn off the *dome* once we enter. That is what worked for us on the way in." *Become one with the universe. One had to allow oneself to be swallowed and claimed by the cosmos. That was the secret to travelling through a black hole.*

"Okay. I understand," said Madhavan.

"But not till the last possible moment. You will have to do it manually just at the right time." Anara felt for and sank back in her chair.

"Join me again?" asked Madhavan.

"By all means. Right behind you." He turned towards Anara. "Break a leg, Captain Anara." Fraser saluted, turned and walked out behind the engineer. Kevin looked at Manisha, finding the same concern in her eyes. He closed his eyes briefly as if capturing her image in his mind forever, smiled wanly, gave her a small wave and stepped out.

"I want to check your eyes one last time, Captain. Do you mind?" requested Dr Khan.

"Sure. We have a few minutes. You need to be near the *dome* with Madhavan."

"Yes. I will be there. Now open your eyes wide," said the Doctor. He peered closely using a few instruments. Once again, there was nothing wrong physiologically. He was stumped.

"Well?"

"No change. I can't find anything wrong with you or with any of the other people."

"I have been thinking about it. I think it is the effect of electromagnetic radiation surrounding us. Just like neutrinos or cosmic rays travel through tons of concrete, so too do the energised particles here. The anti-matter particles may not enter the EM field but other more exotic particles may permeate our atmosphere freely. They might be interfering with the transfer of electrical impulse in my eyes or the neurons in the brains of the afflicted people. The *dome* is keeping them safe. But I don't know what the exposure to the next part of the journey without the *dome* will do to their bodies. You will take care, won't you?"

"Rest assured, I will do the best I can. Let me just put a couple of drops in your eyes to keep them lubricated." He administered the eye drops, gave Anara a quick hug, waved goodbye to Manisha, and left.

"And then there were none! How much further to our next oblivion, Lieutenant?"

25

Oblivion

"I have no visuals yet, Captain. We've only covered a hundred thousand kilometres so far." Manisha turned around in her seat. "Why did you call it 'oblivion'?"

"That's what it feels like. You are seemingly torn from your body, disassembled into the most basic physical particles. You disappear, if only for a few moments. Oblivion sounds appropriate, doesn't it?"

"If you say so, ma'am."

"Keep looking." She settled back. *They would find the exit very shortly. If not, they would die here in a desolate place. 'Zero space'—that's what Ryan had called it. All empty. The ultimate void. A superlative scientific discovery and no one to tell. No one would ever know. Maybe no one back home would be left to know. Oblivion described it accurately.*

"You're monitoring the particle flow, right Narada?"

"Affirm. We are still on the trajectory we plotted, moving away from the black hole. Particle density is down by eighty percent."

"So we continue to go true?"

"Yes. We do. Moving in a straight line."

"This place is like an immense sphere, isn't it? And we do not know whether we are in the centre or a side or if we're going around in circles. How much time do we have left?"

"Endurance twenty-five minutes as per last report."

So, this is how it will end. Far from home. Seven people holding fort. Eighty-nine frozen bodies. I wonder what total annihilation feels like. It will be swift, that's for sure. The EM screen will fail first. Then the antimatter particles will come flooding in towards Antariksh. *The first few particles will be enough to completely obliterate the ship and us. We will cease to exist. No. Even after death there is an essence of the human body left. Some wreckage of the ship. Some remnants of memory. The eternal soul. But here in this universe, there will be nothing leftover. Not a single particle of matter. All is one. I am becoming quite philosophical today.*

"I see something!" Manisha called out, excitedly. "There! Right there! Starboard! Did you see that, Captain?"

Her excitement was infectious. "Unfortunately, I cannot. Narada?"

"I am observing the phenomenon. Apparently, we are no longer moving true to our point of origin. Somewhere in the last few minutes we seem to have strayed by almost fifteen degrees. Correcting course now."

"Madhavan. Colonel Fraser. I hope you can hear this. It appears we are reaching our destination. All ready at the *dome*?"

"Yes, ma'am. We got this." Madhavan's voice came through strong and clear. He was solving a mechanical problem. He was in the zone.

"Narada, keep talking. Let everyone know what you are observing."

"Ten thousand kilometres straight ahead. It is becoming clearer now. It's similar to an accretion disc around a black hole. Only instead of matter, it should be antimatter. Gravitational pull is increasing once more. Captain?"

"Uh huh?"

"I believe we have proof of another scientific theory. Gravity seems weaker over large distances because the gravitons move through baby universes or different dimensions. Gravity goes into this universe from ours and then reappears, seemingly able to travel large distances without losing its pull."

"You know what that means, don't you?" Anara said.

"What?" asked Manisha.

"It means all of the theories Ryan had explained to us before are linked."

"Five thousand metres," reported Narada.

"One last indulgence before we go in, Manisha. Judicious use of our precious minutes before we disappear. Should I explain?"

"That would be helpful, ma'am," Manisha said grateful for anything to take her mind away from the impending doom.

"Black holes are actually worm holes. But instead of directly leading to a different place in the universe, the wormholes open into baby universes or another dimension. And there are other entrances and exits from this place. This universe functions like an orbital flight interchange, or the airport of old. You come in through one gate and you leave through another. If we do manage to exit through a white hole, then that would be the other end of the wormhole, the exit from this place. Only..."

"Only what?"

"Only the other end may not be fixed in our galaxy. It may change or may be difficult to locate once you enter this universe. I know it sounds confusing, but what I'm trying to say is we may find an entrance but not the exit, or the exit may lead us to another even more exotic space."

"And if we do get out into our universe we still do not know where we will end up. Maybe the other end of the galaxy or maybe at our own doorstep on Earth." Anara smiled. "Better note all this down. That will be the second Nobel Prize for people on this ship. And now, back to business! Narada? Status?"

"We are being pulled in just like the previous time at the black hole. Gravity is rising exponentially but it is nowhere near the levels we encountered at the black hole. Minimum reverse settings on our graviton generators should be enough."

"Mr Madhavan, do you copy?"

"Affirmative. We seemed to have gotten lucky. This gravity I can handle with our engines. I'm setting the graviton generators to reverse field and handing over control to Narada. I do hope you will stay online this time, Narada, won't you?"

"I will do my best, sir," Narada replied, unflappable as usual. "I estimate three minutes to entry."

"Execute our plan, Doc." Anara called.

Down near the *dome,* Dr Khan's finger hovered tentatively over the *dome*'s switch. The thought that his action might be committing eighty-nine souls to an inglorious death was daunting. *Well. Here goes nothing!* He pushed the button and the *dome* switched off.

It took just a few seconds after the pods opened for the unearthly screaming to fill the chamber. The noise filtered through the intercom channel and Anara closed her ears. *They are alive and in pain again. So much pain.* She screamed herself.

The space around her seemed to dissolve. She could barely make out the words of comfort coming from the young girl who sat at the control station. Anara screamed and rocked. Darkness surrounded her and then a blazing, shimmering glow filled the ship once more.

All is one at the onset of oblivion.

That was Anara's last thought as she lost consciousness.

All is one.

26

Into The Quantum Foam

There was darkness and then there was light. She did not know if she was awake or dreaming. It was the same this time and yet it was different. Once more she travelled the universe. She saw the beginning and she saw the end. This time she witnessed her death. It was meaningful. She was happy.

And then she was growing smaller. She was smaller than a speck of sand. Smaller than an atom. She was inside her own body. Her blood cells moved in waves around her. She was one with the flow. She grew even smaller. This time she saw a completely different version of the universe, this one at the quantum level. She was now floating in the quantum foam. At that infinitesimal level there were no particles, only energy. Energy in its purest form. Light and dark energy. Light and dark matter. She knew there were two types of matter and now there were two types of energy. It was wondrous to behold. Now she knew the answer! Nature was Yin and Yang. Female and male. Light and dark. Opposites trying to achieve equilibrium. Black hole and white hole. It all made sense now. She was right! Nature always restored balance!

She tried moving her hands. They moved. So did her feet. She could hear quite well. Why were people screaming so hard? She remembered something. She knew these people. Family? Friends? People she knew from another life? Why was the answer eluding her?

At the next moment she remembered. There were people who depended on her.

Flashes. Glimpses. Visions. Was she sleeping or was she awake? It seemed so corporeal even if it was only her imagination. *But I am blind. I can't see. These have to be part of my dream.*

She woke up with a start.

27

The Reversion

The restraints on her chair held her back and she struggled against them, thrashing about till she found the release. She felt the space around her; her fingers met nothing but wisps of cold air. She shivered.

The last thing she remembered was sitting in her chair in Ops as they entered the white hole. Then the flashes of light. And now she was back. *I do hope it is normal space and not another baby universe.*

"Lieutenant Manisha? Narada? Anybody?"

She pushed herself up. *I remember the layout. I can find my way around.* She felt her way to where she remembered Manisha was sitting. She stubbed her toe on the leg of a chair and winced in pain, but at that moment her hand closed on hair. Long hair, tied in a ponytail. It was the Lieutenant with her head fallen back against the headrest.

"Manisha? Wake up. Are you alright?" She shook Manisha gently. The head lolled back, and there was no response. She put her hand to Manisha's nose. *Thank god! She is alive and breathing. Better let her lie where she is.*

"Narada! Damn you. I need you."

She stepped around the Lieutenant's stationary form and found her way to the main door, stopping just in time. *There will be no oxygen outside. I need a breathing mask. It will be cold too. Where did I leave my jacket? I need to find the emergency locker. Where is it? Why is the universe punishing me again and again? I barely make it out of one predicament before I land into another. It has been hours and days of nonstop nightmares now.*

"Give me a break, will you!" she shouted to no one in particular.

She found the locker and opened it. She felt around and found the body suit and breathing mask. It was awkward getting them on, but she managed after some struggle. The control pad on her wrist was tactile. She pressed a few buttons and warmth spread on her body. The filtered air with a higher concentration of oxygen felt good. *Now back to the door and out.*

The corridor was totally silent. She fumbled her way down the stairs to the lower level, feeling her way along the wall.

She reached the *dome* and managed to get the door open. Stepping in, she almost immediately stumbled over a body and lost her balance. Cursing and raising herself to her knees, she felt around with her hands and examined the body. Either the Major or the Colonel, judging by the size of the torso and the holster on the hip, she decided. *Alive and breathing, thankfully.*

Well, I am here. What do I do now? Without sight, without sounds to guide me, I am less than useless.

"Doctor? Ryan? Anybody?" she called out.

Was that a groan?

"Who is it? Ryan? Doctor?" She stumbled further into the *dome* feeling inside each capsule, looking for a moving body. She hit another body on the floor and fell again. The fall was much harder this time. Her head hit the corner of a capsule and she collapsed in a dead faint.

***

When she came to, she had no idea how much time had passed. She sat up gingerly, feeling the bump on her head. Her fingers came back wet. *Blood. Must've cut myself. Doesn't feel too bad. It will have to wait.* She had been in the *dome* many times before but without her sight she was completely disoriented. Pushing herself up to a sitting position, she tried to stand, then groaned as a wave of nausea hit her, and sat back down. She drew her knees to her chest and bent her head, waiting for the feeling to pass. She was grateful for the suit. She could feel the cold on her exposed hands and face, but the suit was keeping her body warm. The mask gurgled as it continued to provide filtered air. She took a few deep breaths, then pushed herself up with the support of the capsule. Waiting for her head to stop spinning, she listened for the groans she had heard earlier. This time the room was completely silent. She felt a small gush of air. She had been wrong. There was fresh air available even if there was no heat. At least some parts of the environment control were working. She shuffled around the capsule and found the feet of the person inside, then made her way to the head. *Long hair, female. Still breathing, but the skin feels quite cold. Who?* She needed to move fast else the people in the capsules would die of hypothermia in the cold environment.

First order of priority—get the power back up. She could function in the dark, but her crew needed oxygen and heat. The tertiary fuel cells might have some juice left. *Will I be able to restart the fusion generators? Will I remember how? It's been so long since my basic engineering training. Where is the useless AI when I need him?* A wave of panic washed over her. "Narada! Ryan!" she screamed, her voice echoing in the vast hall. "Narada?"

She listened intently. There was no reply. On the other hand, she was now able to make out the sound of breathing of dozens of people. *Thank god. Most of the crew seems alive. Why am I the only person awake? Never mind, I have to find my way to the engine room.* "Ryan? Narada?" *It is of no use. Can't waste time here. Time is always my enemy.*

She raised her hands in front of her and, bumping into numerous objects, finally managed to find her way to a wall. Following its curvature, she found the open door of the *dome* and stumbled out gratefully. She had lost precious time in the exercise.

Walk left in the corridor, down the stairs, turn right. Visualizing the way in her mind helped and she eventually reached what she believed was the entrance to Engineering. She felt around the wall and pressed the door panel. No soft swoosh of a door opening. Nothing. She found the handle and tried to slide the door open. It moved with a little effort. In case of power failure, the doors were designed to unlock automatically. *Thank god for small mercies.*

She tried to reorient herself and made her way to the control station. Her hands found a smooth surface. *The controls are off-line. Need to boot up the batteries manually. Where are they located? Right side wall, bottom section. It should slide open. I can do it.* She turned around. *Which way am I facing? The station is here, so the door is on my left. I need to go right.*

A half hour later, having stumbled across the entire section without locating the batteries, she gave up. She sat down with her back to wall, breathing heavily with exertion. She wanted to scream in frustration. She wished someone would come find her. *Someone. Anyone.*

She put her head down. Tears rolled down her cheeks, hot and plentiful. The dam had burst. All her frustration, all her failures came crashing down upon her. She had fought every step of her way. She had not given up. Until today. She couldn't do this anymore. Every person had their limit. She had just reached hers. All her training, the years of preparation, the many voyages in space, none of it mattered anymore. She slid down further against the wall till she was lying on her side. Nestling her head in her hands, she closed her eyes. No more. *Why am I being punished? I tried my best.*

28

Reawakening

The hands against Anara's face felt cold and metallic. She was lifted up effortlessly and laid down in a more comfortable position. *What's happening?* She was too listless to care. *Maybe it is the lack of oxygen playing tricks with my mind.*

It was when a cold towel was pressed against her forehead that she opened her eyes. She caught the hand wielding the towel, rising up to a half-sitting position.

"Who is this?" she asked sharply.

"It is me, S12, Captain Anara. I did not see you in Ops, so I searched around, and found you lying here."

"S12!" Her robot helper was here. She had forgotten all about him. She fell back, relieved. "S12, what's our status?"

“I do not understand the question.”

Of course you don’t. You’re a military robot.

“I meant the status of the ship. Never mind. Help me up, will you? You’re the best option I have right now. You will have to be my eyes and hands. We need to get power and environment working, then we have to go help the crew.”

Holding on to the powerful arms of S12, she rose to her feet.

“Help me find the battery shunt. It should be in the right wall of the room, inside a panel at the bottom. Can you see in the dark?”

“Perfectly well. I have built-in infrared and night vision.” He walked her to the right wall. “There are no panels near the floor, Captain. There are two panels about one-point-five metres above floor level. Are these the ones you are looking for? Which one do you want me to open?”

No wonder I could not find them. I was crawling along the floor while they were just above my head. Stupid mistake.

“Read the labels. Which one says ‘Backup fuel cells’?”

“The one on the right.”

“Open it.”

There were sounds of a handle being pulled.

"There is a control panel inside, but it is offline. There is a lever alongside."

"That's the manual override. Pull it downwards."

"Done." The lights came on.

"Are the lights on?"

"Yes. We have lights."

A small whoosh heralded the arrival of more fresh air from the environment control. *Madhavan must have kept the environment controls on standby.*

"Now we need to restart the fusion generators. Take me to the main station. Centre of the room."

S12 worked rapidly under her instructions to get one fusion generator started up.

"I want to thank you for coming to my assistance. I couldn't have done this without you," she said as she waited for the robot to finish its work.

"That is not necessary. I was just following orders. This is my duty."

"You may have just helped save this ship and ninety-six humans. Duty or not, the crew of *Antariksh* may owe their lives to you." With the environment controls up, she allowed herself a sigh of relief. "What does the energy indicator show?"

"Twenty percent of capacity."

"That's good enough. You can initiate the start-up sequence now to bring the ships controls online."

The robot figured out the sequence to be followed.

"So, how is it, R12, that you were not impaired by our last trip through the white hole? The entire crew and every system on this ship was affected."

"I really could not answer that question, but it may have something to do with the fact that the Colonel disconnected me from the central server and placed me in full autonomous mode. I turned off my power supply when we entered the hole and went into unitary status. That means completely inert. Perhaps that protected my circuits?"

"Lucky for us. Okay, how's the M-AM fuel chamber?"

"45% matter, 15% antimatter. Holding steady."

"Say again? 15% antimatter? That's not possible!"

"It says so right here. 15%," S12 confirmed.

The Lord taketh away and the Lord giveth back. Anara said a silent prayer. They had fuel, it did not matter how.

***

The bright lights of the *dome* revealed a different sight than earlier. Some of the crew had woken up. They sat holding their heads, their legs dangling over the sides of their capsules. Sounds of people in pain filled the room. But they were awake. The effects of the transit through the white hole seemed to be passing.

S12 described the scene to her and led her to where Ryan was sitting on the floor. He looked up as they approached.

"Looks like we made it out, Captain, but you look like something the cat dragged in. What happened to you?" He looked drawn out. His eyes seemed to be sunken yet as sharp as ever.

"A little bit of this and a little bit of that, Ryan." She reached out and found his hands, squeezing them tight. He stood up with her support and pulled her into an embrace. She held him close. It felt good.

"It's probably inappropriate for senior officers to embrace in full public view."

"I don't care. I am ready to hug every person on the crew, including the Colonel. Just don't tell him that." She giggled at the thought. "It has been a rough day, but I'm glad to have you back. How're you doing?"

"Much better, actually. I don't know what happened to me. My mind just snapped." Ryan shook his head, as if to dispel a fog, and shivered. "I don't remember much of what happened, only that I was in a really dark place. I could not think clearly. Something seemed to be screeching inside my brain. It felt as if it would explode. I lost total control. I felt as if my mind was being torn from my body. My body was on fire. I believe I screamed? Scary as hell." His voice reduced to a whisper. "I... I thought I was going to die."

Anara stroked his arm, comforting him. He gained strength from that small gesture.

"But I am back now, so let's get this sorted out and figure out the next steps. Give me a few minutes and then you can brief me fully. In the meantime, let me just check on our people. If they have suffered what I have, they will need help. You wait here. I will be back." He walked off purposefully, gaining strength with each stride. There was work to be done and people to be cared for. Just come out of forced coma and yet thinking first about the people under his command. In the past many years of preparations and the last two missions, she had understood his quiet strength and his mental toughness. Anara was proud of him.

***

Just about an hour later, having organised care for the people still in need of it, Ryan found his way back to Anara, who was now surrounded by a few members of the crew. From the tone of their words floating toward him and the smiling faces, he gathered that the crew was recovering rapidly and enjoying their respite from the hellish events of the last few days. He himself felt stronger with every passing minute. The conversation stopped at his approach.

"Ok, folks. Back to your stations. I need your Captain back in command," he ordered, smiling. As the crew broke away, he took Anara gently by her elbow. "You're going to see the Doc now. We need to get those eyes checked again, and also see if there are any residual effects of our journey through the white hole."

They walked slowly, Ryan acknowledging the greetings of the crew they met on the way, on her behalf. S12 followed behind them.

"What's our status?" she asked.

"We have almost forty percent power back on. I've asked Madhavan to hold it at those levels till we decide our next course of action. Systems are coming back online."

"And the crew?" She asked the dreaded question. "How many more have we lost?"

Ryan did not reply immediately.

"The Doc is checking on them right now. We may have been fortunate since most of us were strapped into the capsules, including your truly. We still have three people in coma, but most of the others have recovered."

Anara said a silent prayer of thanks.

"Except you, of course. The ones who had lost their sight earlier have recovered partial vision. Doc wants to check why it is different with you."

"Yes, about that. There is something you need to know." She told him everything.

***

Dr Khan sat Anara down and started his work. Ryan had explained to him what Anara had admitted to have done. He was seething with anger at her irresponsible behaviour and had finally exploded, spending quite a few minutes telling her his opinion in the choicest of words. Eventually spent he had managed to calm down enough to become clinical.

"I will be checking out your corneas, retina and optic nerve and we'll check out your brain centre—the occipital lobe, okay? I'll compare the results against the previous tests I'd done and against the baseline tests conducted when you came on board. Then let's see if we can find a cure. You'll have to be patient." He chuckled at his pun. "I really don't know what you were thinking."

"I know, Doc and believe me no one is more sorry than I am. It will not happen again." She managed to keep a straight face while the Doctor shook his head in exasperation.

"Ryan? You still there?" Anara called out.

"Yep. Right by your side."

"Who's in Ops?"

"Manisha, the Colonel, Narada. Everything's under control. Don't worry."

"Have you figured out where we landed up this time?"

"First thing I checked. We are back in normal space. *Our* normal, run-of-the-mill universe."

Anara smiled in elation. *We are back! We've escaped another nightmare.*

Ryan patted her shoulder. "Yeah, we can start plotting our next course."

Dr Khan came back and started checking her eyes. *All that these astronauts could think of is their next adventure.* He continued his examination. A couple of minutes later, he put down his instrument and sighed. "Just like last time. There is nothing wrong with your eyes physiologically." He attached a small apparatus to her forehead, then turned to a workstation to monitor the signals. He muttered to himself. "Completely mental. Incredibly irresponsible and... and..."

"Stupid?" she offered, meekly.

"Yes, stupid!" He glared at Ryan, his good humour evaporating, as if holding him responsible for her stupidity. "Now sit still and let me work."

Anara wanted to smile but restrained herself. She changed tack. "Ryan? How're you holding up?"

"Uh," he glanced around to check if anyone else was in earshot, then leaned closer to her. "Quite shaken up, to tell the truth. That time when I collapsed, was one of the worst experiences of my life.

I would not want to go through that ever again." He held her hand and squeezed, "But it's over now. We're safe."

"Are we, Ryan? Are we really safe? The black hole is still out there, right on the solar system's doorstep." It was now her turn. As she accepted the reality her mood changed just like the Doctor's. She was quiet for a moment, but then anger welled up, too strong to contain. "You know, for a time back in there it felt as if the entire universe was conspiring against me. Me, personally! I questioned my choices. I questioned every decision I had made. We took a step forward and two back. There were new obstacles whichever way we turned! We barely made it, Ryan. Barely! And we lost a few good people on the way."

"Calm down, Captain," he said urgently, squeezing her hand reassuringly. He glanced around but no one else seemed to be paying attention to the two of them. "Calm down, please."

Dr Khan walked over. "Everything all right?"

Ryan nodded. "We're fine." He grinned and added, "She didn't like that you called her stupid."

Anara frowned at Ryan, then said to the doctor. "What I did *was* foolish and as I told you I am genuinely sorry."

Dr Khan dismissed her apology. *At least she is alive.* "All right then," he said. "There is nothing wrong with your brain's ability to interpret the signals being transmitted by the optic nerve. You were right, it just seems as if the signals are being scrambled somewhere along the way. I need some time to figure out what should be my next course of action. I have enough data on hand now. You are free to go for now."

"Just like that?"

"Nothing more I can do, unless you want me to hook you up to a prosthesis? I won't recommend that. I still believe we can restore your sight. Okay with you?"

"Sure, Doc, whatever you say. Help me up please, Ryan."

***

"About what you said earlier," started Ryan as they walked down the corridor to Ops, "it would be supremely arrogant to assume the universe is interested in punishing a single individual. I don't believe you are arrogant, Captain, and no one is out to get you. Everyone on this ship has gone through trauma, and you have saved them all. The black hole, the baby universe, even Rawat's death—none of it was your fault. You have done well. I believe in you, but I also need you to stop beating yourself up and focus on getting better and completing this mission."

He is right.

"Yeah. I have been bitter. There will be more to come our way. So might as well buckle up and be prepared, right?" She gave his arm a small squeeze. He was her closest friend and ally.

I can work through this.

29

The Causal Loop

"Good thing you can't see the state of the ship right now," laughed Ryan.

"That bad, huh?"

"Yeah. Remember all that pain you put us through—cleanliness, organisation, efficiency? Well, I'm happy to report all that is out of the window for the next few days till we settle down again. Commander's orders. But seriously, we can't afford to release people to clean up right now. There are much more critical things to be dealt with first."

He guided her inside Ops. "Just don't move around too much and step over this part carefully. There you go." He made frantic motions to Manisha to clear out some of the debris lying conspicuously around. The Colonel smiled at the little pantomime show. He was the only other person in Ops besides Manisha.

"Walk me through the status report, Manisha," Anara ordered. *It is good to be back in my chair like it's just a normal day.* "Where did the white hole drop us?"

"Uh. We are around one AU away from our last noted position outside the event horizon. Looks like the white hole spewed us out more or less on our previous course."

"Your analysis, Ryan?"

"Depends on which news you want to hear first. The good, the bad or the ugly?"

"Three options? Even ugly? We are still not catching a break, are we? Alright then, let's start with the good."

"*Antariksh* is in pretty decent shape, all things considered. We have sufficient power and Madhavan is confident of getting the main engines online in a day or two. He also figured out that the antimatter tanks were not really emptied out when we entered the black hole. Our sensors must have been unable to detect the particle levels."

"The sensors malfunctioned? That's it? All of them? At the same time?"

"Yeah, it would seem so. In any case, the antimatter did not mysteriously reappear on our return. However, a bulk of it drained out due to reasons unknown, probably leakages from the emergency purge manifolds, and since the space outside already had antimatter, our particles just mingled with the rest. In normal space, that much particle leakage would most likely have destroyed us. All of this possibly happened within the first few minutes of us entering the baby universe."

Anara considered this. The emergency purge conduits were used to expel antimatter fuel from the M-AM drive into space outside the EM shield in case of loss of the magnetic fields which kept the particles suspended in vacuum. "I'm not convinced, but if Madhavan believes that is what happened, then we should see what he uncovers. Tell him to keep digging."

"Will do," said Ryan. "Now to the bad. The black hole. It's still out there. We have been able to take some measurements on the basis of the gravitational lensing, and it is more or less the same size as when we entered it."

"And the ugly?"

Her crewmembers looked at one another.

"We seem to have been thrown back in time. The on-board chronometers are off by twenty-seven hours. We checked our position against known star chart markers and locations. The last location buoy we left just outside the Oort cloud? Its chronometer reads twenty-seven hours, nine minutes ahead of us."

"Twenty-seven hours..." Anara said. "Isn't that..."

Ryan nodded. "About the same time that we seem to have spent in the baby universe."

"Imaginary time," said Anara, with a flash of understanding.

"Yeah. When we were inside the baby universe, we actually moved into what physicists call imaginary time, which runs perpendicular to real time. And now that we have come back and joined the real timeline, we are almost at the same instant as when we entered the event horizon."

"So, time for us continued to run as we perceived it—linearly. But outside, here in normal space, time flowed on a different path." *Another physical theory proven. Imaginary time is not actually imaginary or merely a mathematical property. It exists, if only in another dimension.* "We did not time travel, right? We just sort of stepped off our normal time onto another path, and now we are back."

"You're right," agreed Ryan. "However much time we may have spent inside the baby universe, outside it was less than an instant. That might also explain why, while we humans remember every detail of our little jaunt, there is no data in any of our recorders of the entire journey starting from the instant we entered the hole till we came out. Every single record is blank. I suspect that is because time continued to flow linearly in our minds, but the instruments can't work in imaginary time."

It took a minute for Manisha to process this. "Are you saying we have no way of proving we were inside a different dimension except our own collective memory?"

"Yes," said Ryan, "and not just that, it means that others may enter a wormhole in the future using our methods, but they will never be able to bring back any data, any images. Ever. Except, as you say, their collective human memories. The perfect vacation spot, if you ask me. No one will waste time on cameras!"

"Even so, how can we have moved *back* in time?" asked Anara.

"Theoretically, the stronger the gravity, the slower time moves for an object. As we entered the event horizon, time slowed down for us as compared to an observer who was outside the event horizon. I am guessing that when we exited the white hole and away from its gravity, time speeded up, bringing us where we are, at exactly a moment before we entered the event horizon in the first place." Ryan's mind was clearing up. He was ready to tackle these multiple mysteries of physics.

Manisha's eyes widened. "But that would mean..."

Ryan nodded grimly. "That means there are two of us in this space and time right now. Two *Antarikshs* and two of every one of us on the ship."

***

There was a long moment of stunned silence in Ops.

Finally, Ryan spoke in a soft voice. "We have not shared this data with the crew. You and the Ops team are the only ones who know about this."

Anara shook her head. "You were not kidding. This is really ugly."

"I don't understand why you call this ugly," Manisha interjected. "I mean, let's just get over there and tell the... the other *Antariksh* to back off. If they don't enter the black hole, then none of this would ever happen, right?"

"It's not that simple, Manisha," said Anara. She collected her thoughts. *How do I make time paradox explanations simple?* "Do you remember your temporal mechanics classes? Grandfather's paradox? Right? The Colonel may not." She turned a little. "You see, there is a thought experiment. Suppose you were to invent a time machine, then you go back in time and kill your own grandfather. That means you will not be born in the future. If you are not born, then how can you invent a time machine and go back in time to kill your grandfather? So, your grandfather stays alive. Which means you will be born and go back in time. Ad infinitum."

"Wha—? That doesn't even make any sense!" Fraser exclaimed.

"Lots of things about temporal mechanics or time travel don't make sense. Classical physics is simple—every cause has an effect. But in relativistic terms, cause and effect may not flow in one direction. The effect can precede the cause if information travels faster than the speed of light. That is why we travel inside our *dome* whenever *Antariksh* accelerates beyond the speed of light," explained Ryan. "In simple words we cannot assume that our actions in this time will not disrupt the normal flow of events."

"And yet," Anara spoke up, "we cannot just sit by and do nothing."

"Then, we'll have to think about our action pretty fast since the other *Antariksh* should be entering the event horizon any minute now," Ryan pointed out.

"Can you move us in closer?" inquired Anara.

"Not without being detected by them, no."

Anara sat back, lost in thought. The universe was playing with her again, but this time she knew of its plans and would thwart them.

"Maybe it is our karma to be here today at this place and time," she said calmly. Her path was clear.

"Maybe we were meant to be here. You were partially right, Ryan. Maybe the universe was not trying to punish an individual. This was the path we were always meant to follow. This is one more time we have been given a choice. Can we follow through with what I believe is right?"

"And what is the choice you are thinking of making?"

"Destroy the other *Antariksh* as it enters the black hole and halt the singularity right here. Right now…"

"But… but... are you saying we should kill ourselves?" Manisha cried out.

30

The Final Choice

"If we can send a signal and shut down the magnetic fields which hold the matter-antimatter apart, we can cause an uncontrolled explosion, right at the moment *Antariksh* enters the singularity," Ryan said, thinking aloud. "The shockwaves should be enough to disrupt the gravity field, just like a terrestrial explosion throws up objects in the air against the force of gravity. It could create a discontinuity in the forces holding the black hole's mass together and end this." He looked at them with sudden conviction. "It can be done. We can determine the exact time from our ships chronometer. The size of the explosion will be the largest ever seen in this region of space though."

"You're with me then?" Anara wanted his explicit confirmation.

Ryan did not answer for a few moments. "You're not looking at this objectively. You're letting your emotions control your actions."

"You are planning to kill a hundred people! That's murder! How could you even think that?" demanded Manisha.

This was going to be a bit more difficult than Anara had thought. She had made her decision. For her it was technically suicide as well as murder, but then they would still be alive. The very same people on *Antariksh* would live even when the other *Antariksh* and its crew were destroyed in the gigantic explosion. Such were the vagaries of time travel. *You die, and yet you live.*

"If we had the time I would have argued about religion and philosophy and morality with you. But I'm gonna park that for the minute and talk about plain and simple science, okay?"

She got up and stood behind her chair, holding its backrest with both hands. Her sightless eyes could see neither the starlight outside, nor the blue glow from the few lamps lighting Ops. She could not see the pallor on the faces of the people standing around her, appalled at the decision she had made. But she could sense their panic and indecision. If she could have looked them in the eye, she would have shown them her utter conviction in the path she had chosen.

Without her sight, however, she only had her words to persuade them. She had to set them on a path that would ask them to choose their destiny and that of almost two hundred other individuals. There was no time for democracy. The rest of the crew would never know what their officers had done.

"I don't know the exact equations, Ryan, but you know about CTC—closed time curves? The same events will take place again and again and again! If we do nothing right now, then *Antariksh* will enter the black hole once again, we might make the same choices as earlier, and a second *Antariksh* will end up right where we are. If this goes on and on, this space will be filled with an infinite number of ships, doing nothing. Am I right?"

"Yeah. CTC will mean we will relive the same events over and over. There is no end. We will be in a loop."

"Or in a paradox. On the other hand, if we destroy *Antariksh* and that black hole, we will not enter the baby universe, so we will not come back here at this instant and destroy the ship. Once more, we are in a loop. Don't you get it? There are only two constants here in this place and in this time—us and the black hole! One or both of us have to die for us to break the loop."

"But what if you do destroy the other ship and break the causal loop? I mean, once they are destroyed, they will not have entered the other universe, and we will not be here. So, how will we destroy them a second time? The loop would have been broken." Manisha was trying her best to make sense of the whole thing.

"Not necessarily. I think when we moved into imaginary time, the act generated an… an *interrupted* loop," explained Ryan. "One in which we are part of the chain of events and yet we can influence the future without effect on ourselves. The two realities – one before our entry into the black hole and second of our exit from the white hole – are disconnected. That is, the two realities are no longer entangled as cause and effect. The actions we take from this time onwards should theoretically have no effect on *our* specifically you, me and this *Antariksh's* past." He knew temporal mechanics took a huge leap of faith to understand. One needed to throw common logic out of the window and think non-linearly. There was no absolute in the flow of time. It flowed differently for different observers of the same event. In fact, observers affect reality. Ironically, he needed a lot more time to explain all of this to other. Manisha would grasp it faster because of her engineering and space flight background, but the Colonel, though as smart as any other person, would soon be hopelessly lost.

"Still," he continued, "I don't think we can prove any of this until we take some dramatic action in this time. Both *Antariksh* and we need to interact directly with the other ship. Just being present here will not be enough. So, yes, destroying the other ship will count as a dramatic step."

"It would still not make the Captain any less of a murderer!" Manisha refused to give in.

Anara felt tears welling in her eyes. "I am not a murderer, Manisha. I am a blind woman who has been trying to make sense of her life, her choices and the world around her. If we succeed, this ship and its crew would still be alive. Earth would be saved. Our solar system would be safe. One man started this—Jim. I don't think he was even aware that the small device he carried around with him would do more than just destroy a city. He may yet be responsible for destroying an entire civilization!" She stood up straighter. "I ask you now - how should we weigh human lives? One against a thousand? How about a hundred of us against eight billion back on Earth? Do you want to be called murderers and yet save a world, or do you want to stand here waiting for circumstances to take the decision away from you? This is not a question of morals. It is a question whether we choose to save humanity or let it perish. We do not have the time to argue. Decide now."

The three people looked at one another.

"She makes a good point," said Fraser, finally breaking the silence. "I don't claim to have understood all the references, but surely it doesn't hurt to try? I mean, if we live then we can carry out our mission while Earth would remain safe. I'm with you, of course, Captain."

"And what if we fail? What about the four people who died during our journey? Don't they deserve a second chance?" Manisha was adamant.

"If we fail in this attempt, we will still be here, as will the black hole. We will just have another go at it. We have better knowledge about the singularity up to the point we entered it. We can put it to good use and enter the event horizon once more, possibly better prepared than earlier," said Ryan. He was convinced about the physics, if not the philosophy or the morality of the plan.

"I don't agree. Fighting against terrorists, enemy soldiers, and criminals is one thing. Cold-blooded murder is quite another. I will not support you. I cannot do this. I will not do this! We have a duty as officers to save the people serving under our command. We have a duty to act with honour. We cannot kill an entire crew of unsuspecting humans on the other *Antariksh.* Who are we to play God?"

Anara stopped trying to convince her. Time was short and there was work to be done. "So be it, Manisha. I respect your decision. Ryan, your call?"

"Uh. I wish I had more time to think this through." He bowed his head for a few moments, then lifted it again. His path was also clear. "We are not Gods, Manisha, nor are we trying to prove out superiority or moral right to commit murder. But this is a zero-one situation. I'm… I'm with you, Captain."

Anara said a silent prayer. Without Ryan's support she could not have done this. "Then let's prepare the signal we need to send. You can bypass all the codes on the other ship, right?"

"Don't do this, Captain. It's not right!"

"Stand down, Lieutenant," warned the Colonel.

"Your refusal has been noted, Manisha. I will not ask you to follow an order against your sense of morality, but this has to be done. Colonel Fraser, will you please move the Lieutenant away from her station while Ryan takes over?"

The Colonel gently held Manisha and moved her to a side.

Ryan sat down in Manisha's chair and entered some commands. The main display sprang to life. A bright red dot was moving on the display.

"That's *Antariksh* coming into range now. I am bringing Narada online. He can make the necessary calculations. Standby."

"No, don't. Narada's ethical programming may not allow him to support this action," commanded Anara. "Can't you do this on your own?"

"Uh, sure. Give me a moment. The other ship is already here. I don't know if I can do all this in the time available. I am setting up the sequence we need to transmit. We need to get a signal out as soon as possible." His fingers moved rapidly, and numbers and equations flew across the screen.

"It's a black hole event horizon, Ryan. It will absorb your signal and get it to the ship. Nothing comes out but everything will go in."

"Nevertheless, I don't want to take a chance. Ok. I think I've got it," he said as he completed a rough simulation. "Transmitting now." He hit the command key. "Signal transmitted to... *Antariksh*, Captain. It is done."

"Time to move away. Mr Madhavan," Ryan opened the intercom, "new coordinates have been entered. Maximum sub-light speed!"

"You can get Narada back online now. How far do we want to go?" asked Anara.

"As far as possible. If our plan works but the black hole does not absorb the force of the explosion, we will be in real danger. Fortunately, we are already a hundred million miles out. A few more million, for good measure. Sub-light velocity will be enough. There's no way we can get everyone into the *dome* on time especially with all the injured and sick folks. Our standard time dilation protection systems will be enough."

Their *Antariksh* moved away while the other *Antariksh* disappeared from the display. It was extremely gradual in the beginning and then it happened in the blink of an eye. One moment it was there, and the next it was gone.

"I think our signal reached in time. Now we wait." He opened the intercom system and addressed the crew. "This is not a drill. All personnel to their stations, and put on your safety harnesses. We are going to experience some heavy turbulence from a large explosion. Dr Khan, please secure your patients in medical."

Manisha watched the entire performance. The clinical manner in which the deed had been accomplished. It was done and, directly or not, she was a murderer. It had been necessary. She had been powerless to stop it.

"Am I relieved of duty, Captain?" asked Manisha.

Anara was surprised at the question. “No. Of course not. You did not agree with our decision. That is not reason enough to relieve you.”

“Then can I get back to my post?” Manisha said. “I can’t stop you anymore. At least let me help the crew get organised.”

Anara nodded and Fraser released Manisha. She walked to her station and started working on locating the crew.

“All people accounted for. Medical signals that the patients are secure. You guys had better sit down as well.”

“Thank you, Manisha. Let’s talk later, all right?” said Anara calmly as she strapped herself in.

***

The explosion was massive but not quite as spectacular as Ryan had feared. *Antariksh* rocked hard in the shock waves. The sensors and cameras focused on the location turned white for a brief instant, and then the central display came back to life with a full and even display of stars and galaxies.

Anara said a small prayer for the departed souls and hoped they would forgive her for ending their lives so dramatically.

“It’s gone!” Ryan shouted. “The gravitational lensing is gone! Stellar matter is dissipating. We did it! We saved Earth!”

31

Fight Or Flight

It was a few days since they had destroyed the black hole. The crew had been informed of their success, but only five people knew the whole story.

Anara was with Dr Khan again.

"I have studied your condition from every angle, Captain. I want to try out a few radical electrical techniques since the first few did not work. If that fails, then we will have to consider going in surgically."

"You don't know what is going on really, do you, Doc?" Anara was at peace. She had been living with blindness for a few days now and it was her new normal. "Let's hold off the surgery for some time. I don't want you messing inside my head. Just get me some sort of external prosthesis, will you?"

"I will need some time to design one which will work in your particular case. I need to bypass your optic nerve and transmit the signal directly to the occipital lobe. I'll get it done, don't worry. In the meantime, courtesy of the Colonel, S12 has been programmed to take care of you."

"Thanks, Doc. Okay S12, next stop, Ops."

***

No sooner had she stepped into Ops, than Ryan accosted her. "Hey, Cap'n. The ship's ready to move. Have you decided which way you want to proceed?"

"Sort of. Call the Colonel and join me in conference, will you?"

***

"When we started off on this mission, we had not accounted for the disruption caused by the black hole. Be that as it may, we have lost a few days but we are broadly on track. I want to continue to Alpha Centauri, to KifrWyss, to complete our original goal—the capture of the individual known as the 'Chairman'."

"You've got some guts, Captain! A half-cocked ship, a broken-down crew, your own blindness? And you still want to take on a whole planet?" said Fraser, astounded at her audacity.

"My blindness, sir, will not come in the way. Ryan here is more than capable of commanding this vessel. And you are more than capable of handling the military operations on the ground. So, unless, you've got cold feet, yes I am proposing to take on the TrueKif. You don't think we can do it?"

The Colonel did not answer. It was getting more and more difficult to take on a woman who had single-handedly guided them through the deadliest of nature's forces. He waited to hear Ryan's point of view.

Ryan was looking down at the table, slowly drumming his fingers on its surface. He was not looking forward to this one promotion. "Colonel Fraser is right, you know. All this was not part of our mission plan. The black hole incident, I mean. We are low on fuel. Hell, we are fortunate we have any left. Fifteen percent! Just enough to get us back to Earth."

"Or to Alpha Centauri."

"Or to Alpha Centauri," Ryan agreed. "Still a one-way ticket. We condemned a ship full of… us… a few days ago. Do we condemn the same people to their deaths again? Are we not done playing God?" There was sorrow in his voice. "I'm not sure," he announced finally, not meeting her eyes.

Anara was sitting right across from him. She had started to learn to read expressions and emotions from the tone of voice even if she could not see the faces. Ryan was wavering, probably on account of the welfare of the crew. But the stakes were much larger. As the black hole had reminded her, as she had become aware of the danger to Earth, she was realising that she held the key to saving an entire civilization.

"There have been no lasting effects on the crew, except myself, and I am not the core of the mission. You and the crew are. The Colonel and his men of the JITF are. The ship's job is to get them to their destination. If I can find RyHiza, we can get all the fuel we need. Have you forgotten what is at stake? The Chairman was ready to destroy a whole city and kill innumerable people for its revenge. We stopped them once. But if we retreat now, how many times will they attack us again? If we return to Earth we will not be able to come back for at least another year. Do you think RyHiza and the Discat will survive till then? If the Chairman could send mercenaries across millions of miles, all on its own, just imagine what it will manage to do with the might of the whole planet behind it?" She slammed the table. "This is not the time to hesitate. This is the time for action! What have you decided, Colonel Fraser?"

Fraser selected his words carefully. He was still not ready to commit, but Anara's argument had merits. "What you say is true. The actual operation on the ground at KifrWyss was to be executed by my troops and me. *Antariksh* was supposed to be our troop carrier, our transport. Of course, it was also meant to provide limited air engagement, if required. I have lost two of my people, but the rest can pick up the slack. The Captain's role of leading us to RyHiza and the Discat and getting us some help will still work. Yes," he said more confidently, "yes, I think we should go ahead. Logically there is no reason not to, if you can get us to the drop-off point. I'm in. Let's get this over with. What say, Ryan?"

"Oh, what the hell! If the two of you have not had enough so far and want to commit communal suicide, who the hell am I to stand in your way! The Chairman had better watch out for us."

Anara said a silent prayer. She had her allies with her. It was time to finish the operation. It was time for retribution.

EPILOGUE

RyHiza sat with its closest advisors. The Discat was in disarray. A quarter of its leaders had switched sides and joined the Chairman. The war was at a stalemate, but there were reports that the enemy was gearing up for a final push.

It looked out of the windows wearily. The verdant green and blue of the city of Nova Zephyss had been devastated. All that remained were ruins. The daily bombardments from the sky and the terrorist attacks had taken a heavy toll. Half the population had moved out to safer locations in the distant towns and villages. The waterways were choked with debris. There was little food for its people.

"There has been no progress on the eastern front, Ducas," said its aide, using the official title for RyHiza. "Our forces continue to retreat. Very soon the enemy will be at our door. We must plan to abandon the city. It is indefensible. At least, let us shift what is left of the

Discat to a safer location so we may continue the fight."

One year was all the TrueKif had taken to overrun the mighty Vrakss nation, overwhelming RyHiza and the Discat's army. RyHiza detested the doctrine of the TrueKif, but nurtured a grudging admiration for their leader who had raised its own army in complete secrecy. The TrueKif had destroyed the peace gained over many generations, throwing the entire planet into civil war.

I am out of resources. I am out of time. We are out of options. Even if Anara has received my message, she might already be too late to save KifrWyss. And if the mercenaries have been successful on Earth, will she even be able to persuade her government to help an enemy planet?

"We will not abandon Nova Zephyss at any cost. This city stands for justice and the unity of the entire KifrWyss people. If this is to be my grave, then so be it. We will make our last stand here and we will make it now."

***

"The telescopic array on HuZryss has been destroyed as per your orders, my Arch," said PiYena continuing his report. "You were right, disabling it was not enough. We were able to conclusively determine that, despite our efforts in damaging the array, RyHiza still managed to send a signal to Earth. But that is no longer possible for anyone."

"What about the human hostages from HuZryss?" growled the Chairman.

"They are still at our prison compound, back on Voxis. Shall I get them executed?"

"No!" the Chairman thundered. "The forty-seven humans must not come to any harm. When we take over Nova Zephyss, I will personally execute them one by one. Then I will send their heads back to Earth. That will be the last trip ever between the two worlds. Earth and that nation, France, have outlived their usefulness. When are my mercenaries, Jur and Biw, expected back?"

"We have not received any news, my Arch. It will be another few months. My people are looking for them."

"See that they get a hero's welcome, then execute Jim. If he can attack his own people, he can betray me. No loose ends. Once this war is over, we will start our glorious work of building a new society on KifrWyss. From the ashes of Vrakss will rise the new TrueKif nation!"

DEAR READER

If you enjoyed this book, please leave a review on Amazon, Goodreads or your favourite site.

Thank you,
Kumar

COMING SOON

Earth To Centauri: Civil War

A blind captain. A ruthless enemy. An alien planet at war. The final mission.

Captain Anara and her crew limp towards the planet HuZryss in the Alpha Centauri star system. Spaceship *Antariksh* is low on fuel and damaged from its encounter with the black hole.

The world of KifrWyss is in turmoil. Its cities destroyed. Thousands killed in the civil war. Its population desperate for succour. Anara must now take sides in a war which is not her own. She decides to help the Discat and RyHiza against the forces of the enigmatic 'Chairman', leader of the TrueKif terrorists.

Anara must snatch victory from the jaws of defeat. But first, she must make an impossible choice—should she use her nuclear weapons and end the war at the cost of destroying half the planet, or should she instead engage in a stealth mission against the

'Chairman' even if it means asking her crew to make the supreme sacrifice?

The 'Chairman', however, has other plans, none of which involve allowing Anara to leave the planet alive.

GLOSSARY

Light year – The distance that light travels in one year. It takes eight minutes for light to travel from the Sun to the Earth, also referred to as Astronomical Unit or AU.

Faster than Light (FTL) – Nothing can theoretically travel faster than light. However, all science fiction writers assume that this barrier will be broken some day and that man will be able to reach the stars in FTL spaceships like 'Antariksh'.

Alpha Centauri and Proxima Centauri – This is the three star solar system, which is closest to Earth at 4.2 Light years away. It will take us approximately 40 years to reach with current rocket ships.

Proxima B – A planet supposed to exist in the Alpha Centauri star system, which may be suitable to support life.

Voyager 1 – This is a space probe launched by the USA's NASA on September 5, 1977. Part of the Voyager program to study the outer Solar System.

https://voyager.jpl.nasa.gov/

Golden Record – A 12-inch gold-plated copper disk engraved with sounds and images from Earth carried on board Voyager to share details of life on Earth with extraterrestrials.

https://voyager.jpl.nasa.gov/golden-record/

Radio Telescope – A special antenna that sends and receives radio signals from space.

Electromagnetic Waves (EM) –Waves in electromagnetic fields like radio, microwaves, light, etc.

Goldilocks zone – A habitable zone near a star where the temperature and other conditions are suitable for life, like the Earth.

Black Hole – A black hole is a region of spacetime exhibiting gravity so strong that nothing can escape from it, not even light. The theory of general relativity predicts that a sufficiently compact mass can deform spacetime to form a black hole.

Event Horizon – In general relativity, an event horizon is a boundary in spacetime around a black hole from which light cannot escape. It may also be the region where the accretion disc of a black hole forms.

Singularity – According to classical physics theory, at the centre of a black hole the density is infinite because all the matter is compressed into zero volume, a one-dimensional state. Hence the name - singularity.

Anti-matter – Antimatter particles share the same mass as their matter counterparts, but with an opposite electric charge. For example, the positively charged positron, is the antiparticle to the negatively charged electron. When matter and antimatter come into contact they annihilate each other releasing enormous amounts of energy.

Wormhole – A wormhole is a theoretical concept or structure that links two separate points in spacetime much like a tunnel with two ends. Also known as Einstein-Rosen bridges.

Time Dilation – In the theory of special relativity, time slows down for anything that moves. The faster we go, the more time slows down when compared to a clock at rest. Time, therefore, is relative, not absolute.